SCENES
OF A BEST-SELLING
AUTHOR

Michael Krüger was born in Wittgendorf in 1943. He is a distinguished poet, publisher and critic. He has been publisher at Carl Hanser Verlag since 1986 and is editor of the literary magazine *Akzente*. His awards include the prestigious Peter-Huchel-Preis and the Prix Médicis Etranger.

Karen J. Leeder is the author of *Breaking Boundaries: A New Generation of Poets in the GDR* and is a Fellow in German at New College, Oxford.

ALSO BY MICHAEL KRÜGER

At Night, Beneath Trees: Selected Poems
The Man in the Tower: A Novel
Diderot's Cat: Selected Poems
The End of the Novel

Michael Krüger

SCENES FROM THE LIFE OF A BEST-SELLING AUTHOR

TRANSLATED FROM THE GERMAN BY
Karen Leeder

VINTAGE

Published by Vintage 2003

1 3 5 7 9 10 8 6 4 2

Copyright © Sanssouchi Verlag AG Zürich 1998
English translation © The Harvill Press

Michael Krüger has asserted his right under the Copyright,
Designs and Patents Act, 1988 to be identified as the author
of this work

Originally published in Switzerland under the title *Aus dem
Leben eines Erfolgschriftstellers: Geschichten*

First published in Great Britain in 2002 by
The Harvill Press

Vintage
Random House, 20 Vauxhall Bridge Road,
London SW1V 2SA

Random House Australia (Pty) Limited
20 Alfred Street, Milsons Point, Sydney,
New South Wales 2061, Australia

Random House New Zealand Limited
18 Poland Road, Glenfield,
Auckland 10, New Zealand

Random House (Pty) Limited
Endulini, 5A Jubilee Road, Parktown 2193,
South Africa

The Random House Group Limited Reg. No. 954009
www.randomhouse.co.uk

A CIP catalogue record for this book
is available from the British Library

ISBN 0 09 944918 8

Papers used by Random House are natural, recyclable
products made from wood grown in sustainable forests.
The manufacturing processes conform to the environ-
mental regulations of the country of origin.

Printed and bound in Great Britain by
Cox & Wyman Ltd, Reading, Berkshire

For Felicitas Feilhauer

Contents

The Beast

I AM, IF I MAY SAY SO, A SUCCESSFUL WRITER. FOR TWENTY
years now I have been working – neglected or misunderstood
by the critics and envied by anyone who cannot make a living
from their own work – on a chronicle of our family history: 14
volumes so far, if I have counted correctly, which have themselves
been translated into almost every living language, so that, with all
the special issues, paperback and book-club versions, my archive
contains more than 500 different editions of my efforts. I don't
mention these things out of vanity – although the success of
my work all over the world, notwithstanding the critics, might
well have given me grounds – but rather to give a sense of the
context within which my work, and with it my responsibility to
my readers, should be understood.

The not inconsiderable revenue from book sales is divided
among my family. Any living family member with a major
role receives up to 2 per cent of the domestic revenue per
book while those with minor roles get half of that. If a family
member is presented in a particularly unfavourable light, a special
compensatory tariff is agreed, up to 4 per cent of the accrued
book-club revenues at home. For many years my father's sister,

Aunt Hilda, who has been cast as the statutory old dear in all the novels, collected all her royalties in hard currency, so that now, after the collapse of communism, she is the proud owner of a renovated baroque castle in Bohemia. She has also taken over sales in the whole of the former Eastern bloc and Asia. Film and television rights are the province of my brothers, who have offices in Los Angeles and Munich and negotiate favourable television deals via Hungary.

My mother's family looks after the merchandising – mugs bearing pictures of the main characters and T-shirts emblazoned with choice phrases from the novels have proved particularly lucrative. In total about 400 people now make their living directly from my books or from the business ventures established with money from them.

In this way the administration and management of my own rights remain in the hands of the family, at the head of which stands my father, who chairs the board which oversees our global operations but also performs all the honorary functions in my stead: receiving international and any remaining local literary prizes on my behalf, accepting honorary degrees, scrutinising doctorates written about me and running the archive. My role in our little empire is exclusively to write. Because I discovered my own style relatively early – earlier than the unfortunate Kafka, earlier even than the (in economic respects at least) exemplary Thomas Mann – I have never suffered a serious artistic crisis. And since the business of producing a conscientious record (along with necessary artistic embellishments) of any normal family would run to 30 moderately sized volumes, my own rather more extreme family circumstances would have allowed me to continue happily for another twenty years or so with my 300 pages per year, without having to invent a single incident or gesture. Indeed, I would have remained a modest but contented individual, a single man with no particular needs, a man who enjoys life and respects the word, if something had not happened one day which was, quite literally, to change everything overnight, with the result that, for the first time in my life, I am not in the thick of a new episode of my family history but am instead engaged in writing this account.

On publication of my eighth or ninth novel, which, like all its predecessors, enjoyed world-wide success as a book, film and television series, my German publisher at the time made me a gift. With the very best of intentions, and in the mistaken belief that I had been treated unfairly by my family, who he believed frowned on my having a companion of any sort, he gave me a pet. In his rather charming naivety, he could not believe that the business of typing up my novels single-handedly could supplant the need for almost any such companionship. He could not grasp that the labour of drafting my novels, in any case invigorating rather than debilitating, was so important to me precisely because it allowed me to keep my family, if not the rest of humanity, at arm's length. The man who has dedicated himself to Art is lost to humanity.

Nevertheless I accepted his gift, which came in acknowledgement of sales of a million copies (within ten months), although the family would certainly have preferred something more tangible, or a rise in percentage profits. It was a small black animal with a shaggy pelt and black button eyes, about the size of a squirrel, that seemed to feel at home in my study straight away.

I was just about to embark on a long flashback: the fateful marriage of my maternal grandmother to my boorish grandfather — a match destined to prove disastrous in almost every respect — and was cheered by the presence of this comic and undemanding little creature. It scrambled up the walls without difficulty and would hang like a dark stain in the corner of the room. Sometimes it would nestle down inside the lamp and blot out the light. Occasionally it went to ground for days and refused any attempt to coax it out of its hiding place. Then it would reappear out of the blue in my bed and, when I had completed my obligatory three pages and went to draw back the covers, would shoot out from underneath and leave behind a horrible black knot of hair on the sheets.

I would doubtless have got a certain amount of pleasure from this amusing little fellow, which found its way into my novels in the guise of a cat, or sometimes a guinea-pig, but for one terrible thing. It grew. It grew under my very eyes. One minute it was nestling on my shoulder, as light as a feather, nibbling at the hairs on my neck, the next it flopped down like a sack by my knees, and, before I knew it, I was being faced down by a vast and hulking lump that bore no resemblance to the creature I had been given.

First off, the family council tried to establish its sex. Experts were summoned, libraries consulted, the director of the zoo invited to submit a report, but any attempt to get to the bottom of it came to nothing. I took to calling if I wanted to see it, and occasionally it did me the increasingly dubious honour of visiting me at my desk.

At this point it was the size of a sheep, and by the time my mother was born and the marriage of my grandparents had run its predictably disastrous course – the high-point of the fifteenth volume – a hairy monster the size of a yak lay slumped on the floor of my apartment, a panting, wretched thing with a malicious streak that would squeeze itself into a corner groaning, or plant itself clumsily against the door with the most dreadful wails.

There was nothing for it but seek new premises on the outskirts of the city, in an old school-house with an adjacent gymnasium, as things were getting too uncomfortable in the city centre. The postman had started dropping veiled hints; the publisher, to whom I had handed in my resignation, could not refrain from telling his other authors the story; the city council became suspicious when I kept requesting new dustbins to house the unimaginable quantities of dirt; and the neighbours, otherwise sympathetic to the artistic life, drew my attention to the stink which permeated their son's clothes and threatened to disrupt his schooling – a situation which only he seemed to appreciate. Finally I received a visit from a young woman from the Department of Health, whom I had to ask to help me haul the beast away from the front door so she could even enter the flat. A move had become unavoidable.

These days I live in the old school-house and the beast occupies the gymnasium, but regular work is a thing of the past. At all the most critical moments, the decisive scenes demanding total concentration, the beast would start bellowing and there would be no peace until I had stumped up a bucket of water or 10 kilos of raw meat. But because there was no telling any longer where its head was, I had simply taken to thrusting the meat through the nearest window and waiting until the bellowing colossus had hauled itself into position to eat.

In truth the animal presented such a picture of repulsive malice and hopeless moroseness that it sometimes crossed my mind to do away with it. But whenever I had resolved to do the deed and approached the gym armed with a shotgun, the evil-smelling wretch lay rolled up asleep like a huge pile of rotting leaves, so that there was nothing for it but to forget my murderous plans and return to my desk to make a sketch for the next book as quickly as I could.

By now I was managing only half a page a day, which for an author of my standing can only augur ill. There were rumours about my waning creative powers; fundamental doubts about the construction of my work began to surface; the latest doctoral studies from every corner began to assert that my characteristic and confident style, the one constant that defined book after book, was showing signs of sketchiness. The final straw came when the family firm suffered a 20 per cent loss in profits rather than the customary 20 per cent gain, and a crisis meeting was called. A hotel close by was booked for the occasion and reserved exclusively for family members so as to keep uninvited snoopers at bay. In the conference room my father presided, with brothers, nephews and cousins sitting at the table and their families behind them in the second row. Aunt Hilda, who in the meantime had married a stateless Lebanese exile and was pressing for a volume of her own dedicated solely to this adventure, sat opposite and as usual threatened to disrupt the strictly ordered agenda. The agenda itself had only four items. Item one: the approval of the accounts; item two: confirmation of the themes of the next three books and marketing strategy; item three: the beast; item four: AOB.

The first item concluded with the unfortunate realisation that the family business had only managed to avoid going under by dint of some skilful real-estate transactions and some smart dealing in America. The truly alarming discovery was that book sales could only account for 60 per cent of turnover, the remainder coming from real-estate and financial dealing – an insecure basis upon which to build a business in this climate, as my father, turning to me, rather pointedly commented.

The second item ended, as per usual, in terrible arguments when my mother's side of the family, which had packed the left-hand side of the conference table, with the sun behind them, claimed that in view of their unfavourable characterisation in recent novels they deserved a larger settlement than had previously been agreed or, alternatively, a central role in the next book. This led to a violent altercation with my father's side of the family which argued, not unreasonably, that the spirit of uncompromising realism which held together the project as a whole rendered such a demand untenable and tantamount to a distortion of the truth.

Then, at last, it was time for lunch; time too for all kinds of factions and alliances to be built, none of which I witnessed, however, as I was driven back by father's chauffeur to feed the beast, which was already waiting for us when we arrived and greeted us with fearful howls.

At three o'clock precisely we began the process of settling on the cast for the novels to come. Each aunt present at the meeting was given her one great entrance – and a precisely calculated number of minor ones; my mother's cousins and their dreadful wives, idlers and parasites the lot of them, and ugly and pretentious to boot, were to be the focus of the sixteenth volume, which was to recount the crooked machinations by which they had hoped to seize a large part of the family fortune. I wanted to give prominence to one elderly uncle whose nouveau-riche airs and graces had particularly caught my eye, but I couldn't secure the necessary majority for a no holds barred hatchet-job, as it seemed that this uncle, of all people, had been very successful with real-estate in the East. Immediately after the collapse of communism he had bought up all the official residencies in the vicinity of capital cities, chased out the tenants, done up the façades with a lick of paint and sold them on at ten times the asking price – and much more in Prague. If he was to be presented as a villain (and there was also the matter of his Nazi past and a dodgy bankruptcy in Herne during the 1970s which had to be smoothed over with the proceeds of my first book – wonderful material, just crying out to be filmed) then at least wait until after his death. Until then he wanted nothing more, as he reassured us hypocritically, than to be of service to the family firm – not to mention himself, of course, as he drew a monthly salary of 20,000 marks which, when added to various bonuses and dividends, made an annual income of over 350,000 marks.

After novels 17 and 18 had been sketched out so that the proposed link-ups for television serialisation were all in place, item number three could finally be discussed: the beast. The tense atmosphere in the conference room was further strained when the press secretary, a thoroughly unscrupulous journalist who had wormed his way into the family by marriage, brandished and began to pass round an Italian newspaper report about me and the animal, which was full of pernicious and unsavoury innuendo. It even went as far as to imply a relationship between me and the monster which, for its part, was the subject of a double-page colour spread: it lay in a black heap in the gymnasium, surrounded by bars and chains, in one corner of the room a skinned calf, in another a bath-tub which served as a trough. A revolting sight. "The bestselling writer's close personal friend" proclaimed the caption underneath the picture, and there was a shot in the upper right-hand corner of the page of me in a leather apron hauling the bloody corpse of the calf though the window. On the next page another picture showed me sitting at my desk with my head in my hands with the headline: "A writer in crisis?" When the press secretary informed the meeting that the rights to these illegal and covert paparazzi snaps had already been sold to twelve magazines from all over the world, there was such a manifest wave of hostility towards me that my father had no choice but to call on the cause of all this misery to explain himself. I had to stand up and face the barrage of questions, which became increasingly aggressive until they were indistinguishable from out and out attacks. But what could I say in my defence? The beast was still there and continued to grow. Nevertheless, I did manage to cause a minor uproar when I approached the finance committee to set aside investment capital of just over a million marks, for the eventuality that the gym would one day no longer be large enough to house the beast.

Although it was the first time that I had ever requested something over and above my monthly salary – my current dwelling and the gym came out of my own pocket and the daily meat rations were drawn on my personal account – the motion was flatly rejected, with just two abstentions. "We are responsible for marketing your account of our family history, not for your private animal husbandry," came the unanimous opinion. Uncle Richard went one step further: "It is either us or the beast," he said, to storms of applause, at which point even my father rubbed his hands. "Either you return to normal production – three pages a day – and have the animal disposed of," he even used that awful phrase, "or we will relieve you of your responsibility for our family story without further ado."

I asked for time to consider. Coffee was sent for. Aunt Hilda and her Lebanese friend demanded champagne and Uncle Richard, pleased with himself for having polarised everyone so successfully and turning the affair into a full-scale quarrel, ordered a double brandy. The under-eighteens, not yet entitled to vote and whom for the life of me I would not have known from Adam, were given Coke and biscuits. I asked to be driven out to the school-house by my father's chauffeur, where I went to see the beast. It lay in the gym, just as it had done in the magazine shoot, a trembling heap of hair which issued plaintive sighs, as if it knew about the decisions being taken. The chauffeur helped me to lift it slightly, so as to sweep up the filth a little more easily; then I filled the tub with fresh water, and in less than half an hour we were back in the hotel.

The chairman asked for quiet; family members, who for the most part had not seen the animal in years and were relying on rumours to piece together the story, took their seats; the voices fell silent. It was my turn to speak.

What can I say? I decided against the family and for the beast. How I came to this decision, which was to have serious consequences for the rest of my life, I do not rightly know. I can just see myself standing next to my father in front of the meeting, in inner turmoil, but outwardly calm, casting a long, slow glance at the silent family. There they sat, the aunts and uncles, cousins and in-laws, the whole wretched pack of them, staring at me in anticipation: a heap of family history, a pile of filth. I couldn't help laughing. I felt a mighty laughter swell up inside me and break out suddenly, in a shower of dribble. Snorting with laughter as if beside myself, and finally struggling for breath and composure, I proclaimed my decision. The reaction was predictable enough, and yet in its own way quite unique. Chaos. Some people were screaming, others banging on the tables to set the teacups rattling; one uncle charged at me with fists flying, tripped over a child who promptly began to yell, and was immediately poleaxed by its father, the uncle's cousin; and a great aunt fell into a swoon. A fantastic scene – to which one could gladly devote some 12 or 15 pages. I was roundly chastised, my uncle accused of having forced the issue and my father, as chairman, was reproached for not having foreseen the calamity and intervened in time. A heap of wreckage.

As soon as I could I took the opportunity to slip away, went home and threw the beginning of the next novel onto the fire. The lawyers would sort out the rest. I can confirm that, for the duration of copyright, the royalties for the original editions are to be made over to me, which should in any case be enough to keep the ravenous beast and me afloat for a while at least. A special employment programme was devised for the rest of the family, to be financed by the sale of the family business. For the younger members there was the chance of a paid apprenticeship; for the uncles and aunts beyond redeployment there would be free board and lodging in one of the remaining family hotels in Altötting. Interestingly enough, the family attempted to foist our family history onto a ghost-writer, but his meagre stylistic skills were not up to the job of creating an exciting and generally entertaining story. The sorry effort didn't even find a publisher.

For my part, I can stay on in the school-house, as the beast has not, contrary to all expectations, continued to grow. With the help of a shepherd from the neighbourhood I sheared its pelt, cropped it almost to the skin, so that it looks, if no less unappetising, at least a good deal less frightening. And, most importantly, I can see its eyes again, which makes things much easier between us. Negotiations with a circus were broken off, as the beast can't really do anything and there was no demand. Someone would have had to carry it into the ring like a carpet, where it would have lain there, flat and completely motionless – something of an anti-climax after the tightrope walker, and certainly too little for an audience brought up to expect illusion and spectacle. It was even turned down as a filler between acts, and I rejected the idea of having it trained.

I cannot honestly say that I love the beast, but I think I understand it. It has become a part of my life, and perhaps not the worst part either. I have made a start on some illustrations for a book about it, which will appear one day with the publisher who gave me the poor creature in the first place. The contract has been signed.

This testimony will be lodged with my solicitor. I have committed it to paper for the event that a certain part of the family should ever be minded to turn a certain rumour that has reached my ears into fact.

Krumberg, Munich, May 1995

Uncle's Story

O UR FAMILY, UNLIKE OTHER FAMILIES WE KNEW BUT
nonetheless visited, had only one uncle. And even that is an
exaggeration. For while all my friends had, so to speak, an uncle
for every occasion – one for the cinema, one for money, one for
holidays and one for tears – our uncle, according to my mother at
least, was an uncle fit for nothing. He didn't have a proper job, or
a wife; he was stubborn and taciturn, and if we hadn't called him
Uncle it wouldn't have occurred to anyone that he belonged to our
family and was our only uncle. In our family it was the aunts who
ruled the roost. Curiously, they had all either remained spinsters
or were already living it up on their widows' pensions. And for
each of them, all more or less unbearable examples of their ilk,
our poor uncle was a dream come true. None of them was capable
of preparing a meal that would have satisfied the whole family:
one aunt couldn't have salt in her food because of her water on
the leg, while another wouldn't do without it, the third aunt had
to avoid garlic at all costs, the fourth would not touch meat, which
in turn was an essential dietary requirement for the fifth and so
on. In short, because anything that one aunt took into her head
was immediately rejected by all the others our family council,

which we had instituted as a kind of familial upper-house, had decided to award my mother sole jurisdiction in the kitchen and demote the aunts to menial work. The institution of this simple hierarchical structure was anything but simple, however, as the aunts all insisted on their relative social status, the size of their pension and their health being taken into account in the division of kitchen labour. In other words there was constant bickering about the internal hierarchy, and it even came to scuffles. But because they were not permitted upstairs – where my mother ruled her territory with a rod of iron and little concern for the democratic niceties of who should peel potatoes and who should wash dishes – the aunts would repair in unison below stairs. And below stairs: that was Uncle. It was Uncle who was to blame when crockery was smashed, or when the food was over-salted. He was the one who got in the way when dinner was being served, and who had to fetch whatever had been forgotten. It was Uncle's job to take the rubbish out. Sometimes Uncle didn't sit down to his rapidly cooling lunch until after one, because he had been running up and down to the kitchen, and I saw with my own eyes, one afternoon when my parents were away, how the aunts made him serve tea in the living-room with a waistcoat over his white shirt and a tea-towel over his right arm. "You're making it up," said my mother, as I tried to tell her what had happened that evening over supper in the presence of the aunts, but was hardly able to get my story out because I had to keep waiting until Uncle was sent off to the kitchen again for pickled gherkins. The five aunts just giggled, and my father, who had been struck dumb by the horrors of visiting relatives that afternoon, sat grimacing before his liver pâté and waited for the gherkins.

If anyone ever asked why Uncle allowed himself to be treated in this way, they were given to understand that Uncle's white waistcoat was not as spotless as it seemed. That was all anyone ever said. Where the stains might have come from was never discussed, and why someone like my uncle should allow himself to be treated in this way remained a mystery. That my uncle's fate was never mentioned in a family like ours — where everything was always discussed *ad nauseam* and led to endless (according to my mother), unrewarding (so said my father), undignified (pace the aunts), and in any case pointless (me) debates — always struck me as outrageous, but I held my tongue, as it was clearly also important to Uncle to avoid becoming the subject of family arguments. His aim in life was to make himself invisible. He hated being the centre of attention or a burden in any way, but these were ambitions he never realised.

Uncle lived just round the corner, only a street away, in a beautiful old tumble-down house, but came over to our house at lunchtime each day, and all day at weekends, because my mother reckoned that he would starve if left to his own devices. If ever he didn't appear on the dot I would be sent over to fetch him, as he refused point blank to get a telephone. He didn't want to be permanently available. Then again, his door was always open and I could go in without ringing the bell. You only had to visit Uncle's house to understand why he would have starved without my mother's skill in the kitchen. It was crammed from floor to ceiling with books — there wouldn't even have been room for a cabbage. The entrance hall was barricaded with unopened boxes of new books; the kitchen was piled high with folio manuscripts and there were even valuable editions chilling in the old fridge.

He had had a bookcase built above the bath-tub for history; the window in the cloakroom was jammed shut by the small reference library housed on the window-ledge; and the drawing room was completely out of bounds on account of books heaped on the sofa and the armchairs, on the table and the sideboard, and tottering in piles all over the floor. The bedroom was reserved for dictionaries and encyclopaedias, the dressing-room housed philosophy and art history, the stairs up to the first floor were crammed with boxes of rejects whose final resting place was still under consideration. Crammed in the four upstairs rooms were the special collections, which incubated silently in the dark behind closed curtains and occasionally found their way up to the attic when there was no more room. The attics were actually set aside for books which Uncle had in duplicate or wanted to exchange. For in order to satisfy his real hunger, Uncle was forced to part with some duplicate copies, even if, in his opinion, the second, third or fourth edition of a particular work often contained such significant discrepancies as to warrant collection of the full set. He once asked me to compare a late edition of Montaigne's *Essays* with the original and to make a note of all the commas that had been added, because he wanted to write an essay on shifts in punctuation, something he thought would revolutionise scholarship. But because he possessed twenty-four editions of the *Essays* the revolution kept having to be postponed until it, like so many revolutions, became superfluous. Indeed Uncle's literary efforts seemed to consist entirely of plans and projects which had been scribbled on torn scraps of newspaper and tacked up onto the shelves with drawing pins. There were mysterious sketches for minor treatises that were completely incomprehensible to anyone but him ("Utriusque cosmi – but morphologically!"), possible titles ("Tears / Goethe / crying fit, but too late"), sometimes just obscure notes: "threats", for example. But it is not known that Uncle ever published a single word. At least the aunts, after their one and only visit to his house, had never been successful, for all their efforts in the library, in tracking down his name. "He is all talk," they declared, but if ever a description was wrong it was this. For it was indeed almost impossible to get a word out of this strange man, and certainly never any kind of justification or explanation for the fact that he had never published a proper book. When I complained to my mother about the hateful snobbery of my aunts, she would simply say: "Don't worry your head about it, it all has its reasons – its good reasons – and, besides, your aunts can't understand a single word."

Uncle's great oeuvre, the one he had been working on obsessively since he left the university – and it seemed that his dismissal was somehow connected to the stain on his waistcoat – was a *History and Theory of the Typographical Error since Gutenberg*, with various historical *excursi* into the origins of writing. Sometimes he would speak of twelve projected volumes, which, he said, hung round the scrawny neck of his future like mill-stones; at other times he spoke in terms of a slim theoretical volume which would be a slap in the face of traditional philology, while the necessary examples and proofs could be delivered piecemeal and as they were needed. You could do that, he said to me once, with a laugh, and bared huge yellow teeth that were far too big for his skinny frame, but probably came in handy for all that he had to chew, tear, grind and swallow in our family.

Thank goodness he never mentioned that idea again. The

prospect of sitting in that dusty, airless prison hunting down and cataloguing the misprints of world history was, at first glance, anything but enticing, even if the aunts, who had overheard Uncle's suggestion, constantly nagged me to take it on, so that they could at least be certain to inherit the house. "And when Uncle dies" – and they each of them reckoned on him dying before them – "we will clear the house, take all of that scrap paper to the tip, and live the rest of our years in comfort." And I did not even feature any longer in their machinations.

But, for the moment, Uncle's demise was a distant prospect. He sat day after day, and often all night, in one of his first-floor rooms on the hunt for misprints. He had worked his way through Antiquity, all the editions of the Bible, the Middle Ages and eighteenth-century Classicism. The errors from the pamphlets published during the French Revolution alone filled several large banana boxes, to his secret satisfaction, and were to have a dedicated volume of their own. The only friend from his youth with whom he still had any contact, a certain Herr Ritter from Münster, had published a study of the *Meaningful Misprint*, a pioneering work which had not received the recognition it deserved, according to my uncle. The pair of them exchanged long lists of misprints, which would then be incorporated into his own catalogues – all by hand. Of course Uncle's intention was not simply to compile a complete record of all such typographical failings and one day astonish the academic community, which – to his sorrow – seemed to have quite different concerns. His goal was far greater: in a word, he wanted to demonstrate that the entire history of the world in written form was a misunderstanding that rested on misprints. With a meaningful gesture in the direction of the four-metre long blue-bound *Complete Works of Marx and Engels*, which was bristling with page after page of slips of paper, he claimed to be able to prove that the accumulation of misprints in successive editions had resulted in a political superstructure which was destined for imminent collapse. Which of course was true. Mao Tse-tung, too, he considered to be a printing error that had not been caught in time. Modernism was a complete misapprehension based on misprints, and I should be proud that some of the "howlers" in my schoolbooks had found their way into his notebooks, accompanied, in his illegible hand, by a suitable acknowledgement to me as the source. "That will make you famous one of these days," Uncle used to say on these occasions; a fact I doubted, but as he paid me 5 marks for every misprint, I could at least reckon on a certain profit.

So that is how I gradually slipped into the role of Uncle's assistant against my will. After school, during the summer, I would sit in his garden under the Linden tree and read my way through world literature. I earned 400 marks from Dickens, double that from Fontane, and the big Dostoyevsky edition would have netted me more than my father's salary, if Uncle had not introduced a hierarchy of errors. If I simply replaced an incorrect "rest", say, with the correct version "pest", but then tracked down the original "nest", in the future I would only get half the payment, with the result that if I had read the first fifty pages of a book and could see that it offered meagre rewards I would put it aside in favour of something more profitable, such as the early editions of Jules Verne.

My life might have continued in this way. I had almost stopped going to school, instead heading straight over to Uncle's after breakfast. He was developing a new theory which would move beyond his theory of the typographical error to embrace a theory of chance itself. At lunchtime we went over to our house to be terrorised by the aunts, and in the afternoons we continued our patient work. All things considered it was a pleasant enough life, even if I sometimes had the feeling that Uncle was becoming increasingly melancholy. From my table in the garden I would sometimes see his shadow behind the drawn blinds and hear him sighing as if he were bearing the weight of the world on his scrawny shoulders. Or he would suddenly appear squatting on the unopened packing-cases of books in the hall and staring in a trance through the open door and out onto the street, as if fearing that some dreadful misfortune were approaching. At moments like these I felt very sorry for him but could do nothing to help; he didn't want to be helped.

And as it turned out, misfortune did come from the street and walked into the house through the open door. Although I had often advised him to secure the house properly, he had always refused, on the grounds that if the door were locked a thief would get in via the window. I sort of knew what he meant. If the thief chose the cloakroom window, for example, he would inevitably decimate the reference library, to say nothing of the other ground-floor rooms. So the front door remained unlocked and misfortune was free to walk right in.

My uncle owned a car, an old Opel with plush leather seats, that slumbered on undisturbed in the garage – the only place, incidentally, where it was the walls that were cluttered with books. The garage was home to his paperback philosophy collection, which had been assembled in order to trace the passage of typographical errors from the bound editions to the "people's editions" as my grandfather used to call them. The Opel stood there happily enough between Plato and Kierkegaard and all kinds of philosophical histories, each one bristling with a veritable thicket of slips marking the site of some hideous deformation. Why these were the recommended school editions he would never understand. The Opel was seldom used. If truth be told, it served only for Uncle's weekly expedition to the library to fetch the books he had ordered. But there was a catch. The reverse gear had been out of action for more than thirty years. So when Uncle wanted to take the car out, we had to push the monster out onto the street and position it in such a way that he could drive off in a straight line. But Uncle could not really drive, and every time we got the car out all the mothers in the neighbourhood would come flying out of their houses to whisk their children and pets to safety. At times like this I was ashamed of my only uncle, and I was particularly embarrassed on those occasions when he asked me to accompany him to the library. Then I would have to stand by while the Opel screeched into first, scraped up over the curb, or lurched though a red light – to the curses and muttered threats of the angry pedestrians who would smash their fists down on the precious bodywork as it passed. On one occasion when there were no parking-places left at the library which he could drive into forwards, Uncle accidentally turned into a one-way street and into the path of an oncoming lorry. "Get out of the car," he shouted, "quick, out of the car!" We abandoned the car in the middle of the road and took shelter in a porch where we watched a crowd gather round the old Opel and examine it with a professional air, until someone opened the door and sounded the wretched horn.

That was joined by one horn after another until the whole street trembled in a mighty concert. At some point in the proceedings we slipped into the crowd of onlookers and were right on hand to witness how, one after another, the queue of cars laboriously reversed up the one-way street, heading back in the direction they had come from. When the path was finally clear, Uncle simply took the wheel again, to the incredulity of those still there, and lurched off pathetically, practically pushing the lorry in front of him, as if he were entirely in the right.

But things didn't always turn out well. One day as I was sitting in the garden making a note of the fine typos in the old yellow Strindberg edition, I heard a dreadful commotion from the street and immediately afterwards saw Uncle swerve into the garage. A moment later he came running past me towards the house, thin legs collapsing under the weight of all the parcels of books, and paused to look at me for a moment too long, as if he wanted to fix me in his memory. Hardly had he disappeared into the house when the owner of the house opposite came storming into the garden bright red in the face and waving his arms hysterically, demanding to see my uncle who, he said, had left a trail of devastation in his wake.

A trail of devastation? And this was the moment when I made a bad error of judgement for which, to this day, I have not forgiven myself. I went inside with the man, who kept threatening to call the police, and, as there were no chairs without piles of books, I asked him to stand and wait until I had found my uncle. I was going upstairs when I heard what sounded at first like a grumbling noise from downstairs; but it got louder quickly until, as I was standing on the top step, I was overcome by a deafening roar which stopped me in my tracks and caused me to break out in a sweat. It was one of those moments when one instinctively knows that one's life has changed irreversibly. Peering down I saw the man poke at one book with his bony finger, cry out, throw it aside and then seize the next book, fling it open, call out even more loudly and so on until a thick cloud of dust filled the hallway and blocked my view. I had to do something: this man whom I had invited into the house was intent on destroying my uncle's life's-work. With the muffled sound of the folios landing in a heap on the floor and the furious shouting of the man ringing in my ears, I made my way to my uncle's study. Breathing heavily from behind a mountain of filing-card boxes where he had hidden himself, he crouched snivelling and repeating over and over again like a frightened child: "I'm not here, I'm not here, tell them I'm not at home." Which I did. I hurried back downstairs to find the brute in the kitchen library covered in dust, but still engrossed in the same activity. "What a scoundrel," he cried on seeing me. "Your father is an utter scoundrel." By now he was simply tossing books about him willy-nilly until, without warning, he suddenly collapsed into a heap with a whimper and a sigh. I hauled him to the door by his feet and laid him out on the stone step so that he could get some air. At that his family came out to tend to him: his wife, who resembled my Chemnitz aunt to an uncanny degree, and his three squeaky children. There he sat, shrouded in dust, tears in his eyes, gasping for air: a sorry sight.

The man, to conclude this terrible and fateful story, was the director of the library. As he was waiting he had, as was his custom, simply picked up the book closest to hand from Uncle's copious stocks, and realised not only that the book was the property of the town library, but that it had been missing for years and had therefore most likely been stolen, but worse, that the many slivers of paper which protruded visibly from the pages, and which Uncle had clearly intended as bookmarks, had been cut from the title pages of those same books. My uncle, if one were to believe this man, had single-handedly destroyed huge swathes of the county library.

Help was summoned to save the man from an untimely demise. As if on cue, my aunts descended like a swarm of crows to fetch us for dinner, but immediately settled themselves in a circle round the Library Director, as if they were taking part in a seminar, and egged him on as he cursed and raged against my uncle. This from my aunts of all people, who, according to my father, had never read anything more demanding than the magazine *Golden Realm*, and had understood very little of that. Bit by bit all the neighbours appeared until everyone from round about was gathered in my uncle's garden. It looked for all the world like a garden party, and my aunts would have happily served cider and handed round plates of biscuits if they had found any in Uncle's house. If Uncle himself had ventured outside he would have been lynched.

But it was too late for that. For when I finally found a moment to slip away into the house and upstairs to report on what was going on, I discovered Uncle's lifeless body slumped between the filing-card boxes. This man who had taken such great pains never to play any kind of role in the wider world lay curled like a spent question-mark in the dust of his books, so small and miserable and wasted that one could have dismissed him without any difficulty in the briefest of footnotes.

A trail of devastation indeed. Finding his way blocked by a

rubbish-truck and unable to reverse, Uncle had decided to turn the car round in the front garden of the Library Director, and during this manoeuvre had managed to plough the decorative garden fence into the freshly planted borders.

I shall never forget him. And not only because, as time goes on, I become more and more firmly convinced that his reading of history as a web of misprints was right, but also because, however strange he was, I loved him. I would have done anything for him — in any case I would have happily sacrificed all of my aunts put together in order to prolong his life.

tomorrow." And the gentle voice replied, "See you tomorrow. I'm looking forward to it."

I was still standing by the window watching the policemen as they went about their business quite matter-of-factly when the telephone went again. The misunderstanding had been resolved, I thought to myself with a sigh of relief, but let it ring a little longer before I answered. "Who's that?" I asked, and the theatre manager enquired whether I would like to take on a small part that night and the next. "Of course," I said, "see you soon." And I hung up.

I felt miserable. Instead of looking forward to an unexpected adventure, I slumped morosely into a chair and sat contemplating a conundrum with no apparent solution. I still had the voice in my ear; it crept from there through my body and back to my ear, like a worm burrowing its way through me, wreaking its invisible destruction, slowly consuming me from inside, so that I seemed to consist only of dried-up skin. I jumped up in a panic, stripped off at once and stood under the shower for a long time to wash the voice away.

On the way to work the next day, I read in the paper that 250,000 people were expected to arrive in the city for Green Week, the largest agricultural show in Europe. Our publishing house had a stand there, and I had to take a car-full of books over early that morning: the standard reference works on artificial insemination, the birds of Europe, and especially our new best-seller on balcony-gardening, which Berliners had bought in droves in the hope of growing their own personal miniature jungle for their one-bedroom flats. It smelt good in the exhibition halls, a mixture of oil, bird-seed and cow-pens; the animals stood impassively as people came by and pawed at them, and each country had its own stand where there were various nibbles and items of local produce served by girls in national costume. My colleague and I had just been enjoying some very fine cheese served up by a red-cheeked Dutch girl in a lace cap and clogs when I saw a familiar figure in the aisle, hobbling towards me, armed with bags and umbrellas, and one of her improbable hats perched on her head: one of my aunts, an extermination squad intent on execution. There was nothing left for my unwitting colleague and I but to flee Holland without delay.

At six o'clock, having finally made a decision about the evening ahead of me, I took the train into town; by seven I was in the box-office, in my stage make-up and costume, an unexceptional and slightly shabby double-breasted suit with a large spotted tie, selling tickets and taking coats; at ten to eight a woman stood before me with a suitcase in her hand and asked for a ticket that had been reserved for Margit Schneider – which meant that I at least knew her name; at five past eight the performance began and played without an interval until twenty to ten, when it was seen off with a bout of unenthusiastic applause; five minutes later, in our tiny foyer, I was standing opposite the woman with the suitcase who had taken the only chair, and said in a tiny choked voice the sentence I had found in my favourite philosopher and learned by heart: "At last you have found me, now all that matters is losing me again."

The woman, who had seen me on stage a moment before, half got up and replied with a wry smile that she was waiting for Herr Weber who was due any minute, and that she had enjoyed the play very much. It was terribly amusing, she said, very funny indeed, but with that she gave me a strange look, as if it were slowly dawning on her that the final act of the absurdist drama she had just seen was about to be played out in her own life. I clasped her hand, introduced myself, and confessed all. But as she evidently thought it improper to ring Herr Weber at such a late hour to ask for a bed for the night, she accepted my invitation to dinner.

In a local pub of the sort frequented by Berlin artists and known for its miserable, if not completely inedible, food I ate what was to become the longest supper of my life. Margit, as I came to know and address her (even though I detested the name), seemed to have no qualms about telling me the story of her life in public; and far from being inhibited by the presence of a stranger was, if anything, quite the opposite. And as her story unfolded I, who had grown up in the city and was used to outlandish stories from the theatre, was reduced to gaping like some country bumpkin, whereas she, who had been born in a village in the Eiffel and after years of travelling had returned there, gave the impression she had been through all the miseries the world had to offer and come out the other side. Even though she was only ten years older than me, she already had two marriages behind her: one in Cologne, where she had fallen into the clutches of a painter who had given up painting, and one in Paris, where she had married the gallery-owner who, because he held her responsible for the fact that the painter had given up painting, carried on behind her back and regularly knocked her around.

She had travelled through the Middle East with an Egyptian because she became interested in Islam but, after a brief spell in jail on drugs charges, was extradited and promptly fell for the

German Embassy official who had campaigned for her release. She moved with him to Belgrade when his tour of duty sent him there but found that the diplomatic climate did not agree with her and, after a holiday in Stockholm, decided not to return to the dusty summer heat of Belgrade but travelled instead with the aforementioned Weber, a writer who had been reading at the Goethe Institute in Stockholm, to his house in the South of France. Weber was the one: Weber with his books; Weber with his garden, a stone's-throw from Arles; Weber's hands and hair; his modesty and his authority. I hung on Margit's every word, gazing at her mouth which constantly formed and reformed surprising shapes, a few inches from my own, desperate to know why Weber had left her or she him. But we obviously hadn't got to that point yet. In any case: after she and Weber separated, she returned to her village in the Eiffel and took over the farm her father had kept before he died, a dairy farm – which was also the reason that she had to visit the Green Week show. And with the same concentration and attention to detail that she had told me the ludicrous story of her irresponsible affairs she now informed me about new milking systems, an automated food trough, and a revolutionary method of constructing stalls to oblige the cows to lift themselves up to get at their feed, thus preventing the weakening of the bones, a particular problem in the Eiffel on account of the prescribed industrial feed. In the midst of all these technical innovations Weber's name kept popping up as if he were somehow the touchstone for her restless centrifugal energies.

The longer it all went on the more uncomfortable I became. The waiter had lit a candle at our table and the rest of the room was swallowed in shadow. I stared at the woman. She talked, and as she talked she occasionally tapped my hand or poked it with one finger to bring me back to the story. Now and again she even grasped one of my hands – which now seemed quite separate from the rest of me – and pressed it against her lips, until finally, as the climax to this unspoken but irreproachable escalation of physical contact, she paused behind me on her way back from the lavatory, took my head in her hands and pressed it to her breast long and hard, with the result that – already numbed by alcohol, tobacco and exhaustion – I began to sob. "Don't think", came the gentle voice from behind me – as she leant forward with her hands on my shoulders and whispered into my ear (which reminded me immediately of our first and only telephone conversation) – "don't think too much about Weber." And just as I was thinking to myself that it should actually have been me – whether out of pride or cussedness – who should have said this to her, I felt her, to my not inconsiderable relief, lean forward and plant a kiss on my head.

She stayed with me. While I was at work she visited the agricultural exhibits, and in the evening she would pick me up from the theatre and regale me with further chapters from her extraordinary life before we fell asleep on my mattress. Sometimes, when I couldn't sleep, I would watch her in the light of the street-lamp and had the impression that she kept talking even in her dreams, as her lips would constantly move and twitch, as if she were vainly trying to keep the words back until morning. Then I would prop myself up on my elbow and hold an ear to her mouth and listen to the silent monologue.

On the fourth day she didn't show up at the theatre as usual. After the show I went to our usual pub where the waiter, who reckoned he knew our habits, had laid the table and put out a reserved sign. I tried to put off the journey home for as long as possible, drank too much, wandered round for hours, and when I finally collapsed onto the mattress in the early hours in a flat that seemed strangely empty and contained no trace of any of her things, I found a note written on a page torn out of a book: "Now you will have to save your own life for a change. M."

But, of course, there was no hope of being saved.

My Sister's Boyfriend

IN ORDER TO CELEBRATE PASSING HER SCHOOL LEAVING
exams, my sister was allowed to bring her first boyfriend
home to visit. And because one of my most indiscreet aunts had
immediately asked how this boyfriend of hers earned a living, we
were at least prepared for the encounter. This chap was a poet.
At that time we lived in a city that evinced a certain sympathy
for poets: a fact which led to an increasing influx of the same,
with the result that in some circles it was almost impossible not
to come across one. Admittedly none of them had got as far as
us yet, but there were already two in the neighbourhood, whom
we would sometimes spot shopping in the local delicatessen
"Feinkost-Dietrich". One was a Pole with a penchant for Italian
red wine; the other had come from Ireland and preferred French
white. However, notwithstanding such proximity, since our little
family (along with the accumulated aunts who had moved in at
one point or another) was a respectable bourgeois one – my
father worked for the Post Office – no one had the faintest
idea what a poet might get up to when he was not buying wine
at Dietrich's, so we looked forward to meeting my sister's poet
friend with some curiosity. While my aunts considered poetry

as a more or less insalubrious enterprise which would certainly never stand up to close scrutiny, my mother was able to muster a certain respect for the business, given that the young man in question had been enticed to Berlin by a bursary from the City Council – that is, from a body not dissimilar to the one which paid my father's wages. He, it must be said, protested vehemently about being compared to a poet. "Which point of the pay scale is he on then?" he spluttered into his soup over lunch and only calmed down after my sister had patiently explained that poets paid by the city received only a single, one-off bursary and had no pension rights.

The young man who was ushered into our living room on my sister's arm that evening looked much more like my father had done as a young man than the two poets who lived nearby. Squeezed between the aunt from Jena and the one from Zeitz, he looked so disappointingly ordinary that we were ready to resume our normal programme of family bickering in no time, but the poet – who rejoiced in the, as the family agreed, singularly un-poetic name of Knut and, to the astonishment of all of us, actually wanted us to call him Knut – this Knut, who obviously had a highly developed dramatic sense of the sort which appeared to be the norm in his circles, suddenly prised himself out from between the mighty thighs of my aunts and, with a sort of gurgling sound, made a lunge for the cream tart my sister had just brought in and was meant as dessert for the whole family. "He really is a poet, that Knut chap," said the aunt from Zeitz who, being ignorant of poetic tradition, considered the slavering consumption of cream gâteaux to be an incontrovertible sign of poetic talent. After this unprepossessing display my father retired ostentatiously to bed, my mother fell silent and fell asleep shortly after in her armchair, and the neighbours and my sister's friends who had, all in all, been expecting rather more, disappeared without a word – leaving the aunts, my brothers, my sisters and me alone with the poet.

What happened next must be reckoned among the most memorable experiences of my youth. The poet Knut, who was drunk by now, sat in my father's chair, dripping with sweat, with a bottle of Verpoorten egg liqueur swiped from the iron reserves of my Chemnitz aunt in his left hand and a liqueur glass in his right. This he continually filled and drank down in one, and so passed the entire night, until the sun came up, talking about how he imagined the poetic profession, or rather the poetic existence. And truly it was impressive, the way he emptied the glass before re-filling it. He would halt mid-sentence – a typical sentence might begin "As you'll find if you look at Hölderlin . . ." – and stare forlornly at the glass held up in front of his face; then a moment later his pale, flaccid, almost bloodless tongue would slither out and stuff itself into the tiny glass like a sponge, where he would slurp it round until every drop of the dreadful drink had disappeared, at which point he would put the bottle down and proceed to use both hands (thank goodness always successfully) to disengage the glass from the end of his now white-coloured tongue – where the suction held it fast. When this had been achieved and the sponge-tongue was stowed away he would take the bottle again, pour himself another glass and pick up the unfinished sentence about Hölderlin as if nothing had happened. After each of these unpleasant, although curiously compelling, operations, my brother and I would glance over at my sister with some concern, because we knew that this flaccid tongue had not been brought into our house to be stuffed into liqueur glasses.

The first precondition of a modern poetic existence as described to us by Knut was the absolute prohibition on publishing. It was naturally left to one of my aunts to respond by asking whether Knut thought my sister would ever put up with him, a not inappropriate question, we thought, although he did not deign to respond. Secondly – and here, of course, I am giving only the gist of his somewhat rambling theory – the modern poet should find himself a particular field, a sort of nameless structure, or at least a structure unburdened with expectations, and construct it around him in order to make him immune to gossip on the one hand and to silence on the other. When this is done, he can (and this is the third thing), spend the rest of his life extending and elaborating this field or structure in line with his own inclination and ability. It was nevertheless, as Knut assured us, perfectly permissible, later in life, to count the various acceptance speeches given on receipt of poetry prizes as part of one's oeuvre without endangering the substance. We naturally found that reassuring, especially my sister, who could at last imagine what her future husband's work might one day be like. For, in accordance with his theory, Knut had not yet published a volume of poetry. He had, nevertheless, been awarded any number of prizes for promising young writers and had given a whole series of elaborate acceptance speeches, copies of which he promised to send my aunts since they, as is their wont, had dared to question, amidst much giggling, whether it was possible to win poetry prizes in West Germany without having written a word.

It was, as I have already said, a remarkable evening, ending with the first light of dawn. My sister did not marry Knut after all but found herself instead a railway sleeping-car attendant with a drinking problem, who often alighted at the wrong station and would be picked up wandering aimlessly through various cities — a failing which at least meant that my sister got to see something of the world.

The Neighbour

THE HOUSE NEXT DOOR WAS LARGE AND OVERGROWN with ivy and looked like a shapeless woman in a tight green dress with a red slate hat perched on her head. In it lived a widower with his two daughters. His wife (and mother of the girls) had, in an access of melancholy, dissolved a bottle of sleeping tablets in her tooth-mug and swallowed down this unhappy mixture on an empty stomach. The children summoned the emergency services, but all they could do was confirm their mother's death. No sooner had the ambulance disappeared than the children, whose father was away on business, came round to our house to tell us the news and to ask for advice. They were wearing thin summer dresses that seemed to shiver on their skin, as if there were a cold draught in our lounge, and looked from one person to another with an air of desperation. We all lowered our eyes, although the sight of the girls would ordinarily have transfixed us. I imagined our dead neighbour exactly as I had seen her that very afternoon on my way back from school, sitting in the garden in a deck chair, so sad and so beautiful, but for some reason I couldn't picture her face. It was always my mother I saw; or, more precisely, my mother's face attached to the body of our neighbour. When the silence and the endless shivering became unbearable, my parents got up with a sigh to go next door, leaving the two girls in the lounge, creatures from another planet. I had been told to turn off the radio by my aunts, who said it was not seemly to listen to the gathering intensity of Ravel's *Bolero* in the presence of death, and since I was standing up I was promptly sent into the kitchen to fetch apple juice for the girls. But once in the kitchen I suddenly couldn't remember what I had come in for and looked out of the window in a daze. With a start I noticed the light go on in the neighbours' house and a moment later I saw my mother standing in the room, quite naturally, as if she had always been at home there. When my father's blue shirt also appeared, I held my breath involuntarily, terrified of being seen. A moment later my father turned and began to gesticulate wildly, as if he were making some kind of grave reproach and trying to reinforce it with his gestures. But then, from one moment to the next, as if the steam had suddenly gone out of him, his arms fell to his sides and his head drooped. With my mother in tow, he walked out and into the next room where the children said that their mother, our neighbour, had been found.

The moment my parents disappeared from the lit room I remembered the juice. I fetched a bottle from the larder, got down two glasses from the cupboard and returned to the living room, only to find the family lined up and staring at me strangely, as if to imply I had something to do with the suicide of our neighbour's wife. I remember having to touch the older of the two girls gently on the shoulder to make her realise I was standing there with the glass of juice, which she then took in both hands and drank down in a single draught. I will never forget the feeling as the tips of my fingers brushed her trembling skin.

That next day the girls had to start getting used to growing up without their mother, and her husband, our neighbour, was left asking himself whether he had been partly responsible for the death of his wife. You could see how this thought tormented him: the creases around his mouth and on his forehead etched themselves deeper into his skin and looked like gashes that fate, in a fit of rage, had cut into his face. Our adjoining gardens meant that we knew a good deal about our neighbours. Hardly a day went by without some member of our vast family having something to report. My aunts, all of them wily gossip-mongers, were in total agreement on one thing: the man had more or less driven his wife to her grave. At suppertime they would sit, armed with knives and forks, dissecting and prodding and hacking away at the whole thing until there was nothing left on the plates but bloody scraps. Only my parents remained remarkably silent. Quite often my father would become visibly more stony-faced, until he would suddenly slam his bare hand down on the table and shout "Silence!" Our mother, who often chatted with our neighbour over the garden fence, seemed to turn her thoughts inward, as if she might find the key to the whole drama in her own heart. It was her idea, too, to ask the girls if they wanted to come away with us to a rented house in Amrum over the summer. Their mother had died in June, and the holidays began in July. And so it was, to the surprise of us children, that the girls and their father accompanied us to Amrum while my father stayed behind to finish off some work before coming to join us two weeks later.

They were the strangest holidays I have ever had. Our little wooden house, with its musty smell of mouldering mattresses and the walls covered with mildew of every hue, was so flimsily constructed that there was nothing for it but to creep around on tiptoes. It stood between the beach and a little fishing harbour on a spit of land. My mother shared a room with my sister on the first floor, our neighbour slept next door, and the girls were on the ground floor next to my brother and me. At night you could hear the murmuring of the waves and the excited whispering of the couples who slipped past our house to the end of the promontory, thinking no one could see them. Once, when the whispering turned into a din of whimpering cries which seemed to go on forever, I leaned out of the window to make sure I caught every detail, and saw the sisters next door also craning their necks out into the night air.

My elder brother had taken pains to come up with all sorts of entertainments to keep the sisters' minds off their mother's death. He would go out early with one of them to collect mussels or sunbathe, and they would return happy and exhausted for breakfast. Afterwards he would go to the beach and rub them with Nivea, something he did most conscientiously and with a peculiar dedication to the most hidden places, which, he claimed, the sun would seek out especially. In the afternoons he brushed the sand out of their hair and in the evenings he would disappear with one of them to look at the phosphorescence in the water, or the flying fish, which, he said, only showed off their acrobatics after dark. Sometimes he even looked after the girls at night and went into their room, pillow tucked under his arm, to swat mosquitoes. There were a lot of mosquitoes that summer. I was not left out of the fun and, as his assistant so to speak, was sometimes permitted to lend a hand and take charge of the other sister, who of course grew lonely in his absence and craved some kind of attention herself. I was, if I may say so, a good pupil.

My mother seemed to be enjoying the holidays too. Our neighbour, the widower, did everything he could to make her happy. They had hired one of the big basket chairs for the beach, with the number 43 painted on in red, and made themselves comfortable huddled up inside it together. When we had swum quite far out we would sometimes look back to see them sitting contentedly, as thick as thieves together, or clinging onto each other with their arms and legs as the basket began to rock back and forward. Sometimes in the evenings they would go out for a meal and leave us on our own, so that we could have a good natter without being disturbed, and they would come back late so as not to wake us. In the mornings there would then be an empty wine bottle on the white wooden table on the veranda, with two glasses and wasps drowsily guzzling at the dregs. Once I found a cigarette butt with lipstick on in the ashtray and concluded that our neighbour must have been teaching my mother to smoke. She too was evidently a quick learner. In any case her efforts often left her animated and slightly out of breath, and as she stood in the kitchen preparing our meals with much sighing, she would often sing the arias from all the great operas that my father had taught her during the course of their long years of marriage. Only my sister missed out on the fun. When we were on the beach and local boys came over to our sandcastle to admire the three girls, my brother would see them off, saying they were too stupid for our sister – even if they came bearing a bottle of Coke. And if she ever invited a boy over to join us, so that we couldn't get rid of him just like that, my brother would take him so relentlessly to task that he would soon push off of his own accord and leave my sister behind.

But all in all they were two exhausting, exhilarating, wonderful weeks and we owed them, indirectly at least, to the death of our neighbour's wife, the girls' mother. And then my father arrived. His body was white and his face grey – and this greyness cast its shadow over our holiday. My sister was dispatched to join the two girls downstairs, much to the disgust of my brother, and my mother was left to make the best of it upstairs with the two men – something she patently found less than easy. In any case she no longer sang as she prepared the meals, and the light disappeared from her face. From the water we could see my father sitting in the beach chair with a newspaper over his face and my mother on the sand nearby like a bird who has been pushed out of the nest. Our neighbour was nowhere to be seen.

On the third evening after my father's arrival there was a dreadful argument. We were already upstairs in bed – my brother had given up his nightly excursions – and we were listening to the waves and the drone of the mosquitoes when suddenly our neighbour's voice shattered the quiet. As the terrace, where the altercation took place, was at the back of the house we couldn't follow all the details of the argument, but one of our neighbour's remarks came crashing into our room like a bolt of lightning: "If it weren't for you she would still be alive," which he repeated several times, getting quieter and quieter each time, like a fading echo: still be alive, alive . . . Those were the last words we heard as we hid fearfully under the covers in the dark.

The next morning our neighbour and his daughters packed

their things and left the house. My mother sat in the kitchen crying; my father retired to the beach with his newspaper, and my brother knelt moodily at the water's edge throwing stones into the sea. I helped the sisters pack their cases and was rewarded with a heartfelt kiss that sent a shiver down my spine. Only my sister seemed to be pleased by the turn of events that had shaken our house and family to the core. And she had every reason. From now on she had the sisters' room to herself.

The Bluebeard Trust

SHORTLY BEFORE MY TWENTIETH BIRTHDAY, I HAD THE misfortune to learn that the man I had called father for as long as I could remember was not my father. I found out by chance.

The man who had always answered to that name lay down one bright afternoon on the sofa in our living room, read a few lines of Fontane's novel *The Stechlin*, cleared his throat and promptly died. "Your father is dead," said my mother, who probably was my real mother even if we seemed more unlike than like: "he died of idleness." She didn't seem in the least bothered by this untoward turn of events – the death of a man with whom she had, after all, shared a house and a bed for almost twenty years. My father was dead. There was a perfunctory burial service attended by all the neighbours from our wealthy Munich suburb: businessmen, retired sportsmen, officials and a few of the younger relatives who played bridge and tennis with my mother. Afterwards there was a lengthy wake for the inner circle: mother, her two brothers, Adolf and Kurt, and me. No other relations had turned up, if such relations existed, and in any case I could not remember ever having met any other family members apart from the uncles, who had never married or had any children. Mother and her somewhat vulgar brothers were forever huddling together, whispering and smirking among themselves, so my father and I never had the chance to become part of their self-sufficient little clique. To be honest, this rejection didn't bother us too much. "As long as they don't live under this roof," my father would often say, when the three of them disappeared off to the wooden three-seater swing in the garden, "that miserable rabble can do what they like. Just don't get too close," he would growl from behind his novel, and I fell in with him without ever asking whether he included my mother in the word "rabble". We effectively lived like two separate families whom fate had unkindly thrown together.

At the wake, as so often on such occasions, the only topic of conversation was money, discussed in a tone quite devoid of the flirtatious teasing that normally characterised the trio's chatter. The gist of it all was that my two uncles, wasters and blusterers through and through, demanded some part of my mother's inheritance in recognition of the fact – as they remonstrated loudly – that without their, my uncles', help, she, my mother, would not even be alive. "He would have killed you," screeched Uncle Adolf, the more unpleasant of the two, at such a volume that the waiting staff, who had just appeared to serve us pike dumplings, backed out smartly through the swinging door. And Uncle Kurt made a gesture with his forefinger that left no doubt as to my father's unsavoury intentions. He drew his fleshy finger slowly across his Adam's apple.

It was not exactly what you would call a dignified lunch in memory of the dear departed. "Father wanted to kill you?" I turned to my mother in her inappropriately gaudy outfit and asked in shock, for I could scarcely imagine that someone as inoffensive as my father would be capable of such a thing. He had been a slightly shambling but good-natured man, lazy to a fault, who lived off his not inconsiderable fortune – the provenance of which we were never allowed to enquire. He was rich and bone-idle, but never made any great song and dance about it. In the afternoon he would take a little glass of egg liqueur – a parlous offence against good taste, according to the uncles – and in the evening a bottle of wine. In between he would lie on the sofa reading, as if he had not a care in the world. He scarcely seemed to exist, he was so inconspicuous next to my mother, who was the opposite in every respect. There was no doubt about who wore the trousers in our house. She was choleric and grasping, self-opinionated and cold, forever yelling at the staff, who responded by becoming more and more like my father. In short she was a quite extraordinary woman who was better avoided at all costs. Even I kept any contact between us to the bare minimum, although at the bottom of her bottomless heart she may, I dare say, even have loved me.

"Why did my father want to kill you?" I said once more, as an ominous silence had fallen, which was quite out of keeping with the usual rowdy behaviour of my mother and her cronies.

"Not that father," she replied in a strangely throttled voice, "your other father. The lecherous deceiver who left us this house – to which your uncles now want to lay claim. You will understand it all one day."

I understood nothing, but it was fairly clear that my father was not my father and that I was the son of a lecherous deceiver. And since it seemed to be a complicated matter in many respects, I asked for a step by step explanation. The story that emerged, bit by bit but without any trace of remorse, sounded at first like a ludicrous fiction, but before evening had fallen my whole world had been torn to shreds and threatened to fall apart completely.

My mother, as the three of them recounted in unison, was the daughter of a farmer from the Dresden area, and had married a wealthy land owner during the last years of the War. He was a kind of squire, Uncle Kurt assured us, a proper toff, and she became pregnant almost immediately "with you," interjected Uncle Adolf, "you are the son of a nobleman." But a nobleman, my mother continued, who had not only been married five times before, a fact which my by all accounts rather naive mother had not known when they were married, but moreover, he was still married to another woman at the time of the wedding – a lady of some rank, Uncle Adolf chipped in. And for that reason the marriage to my mother would have been considered null and void if, in the confusion of the final days of the War, morality and decency had not all gone to pot. A bigamist and a lecher, my mother concluded, and you are his son.

"Our sister was dishonoured," Uncle Adolf concluded in a satisfied tone, "and it fell to us to restore her honour." "It was our task," Uncle Kurt responded, "but not only our task: it was our duty and our unhappy obligation."

How exactly, indeed whether, this lost honour had ever been restored was never reported by my thoroughly dishonourable uncles. To cut a long story short, my mother, still pregnant, married the man whom I had never had cause to doubt was my father, a cheerful but simple soul who had been drawn into the machinations of the three of them, and for his part clearly had no objection to coming by a house and a son with such little effort. The joke in all this sorry episode was that my progenitor and real father had signed over a substantial part of his fortune to my mother – either of his own free will or under duress – before fleeing to Switzerland, where shares invested prudently in the arms industry had generated a yearly capital that afforded us an eminently comfortable life-style. My uncles now asserted that they had in fact been the authors of our wealth and that after the death of my step-father, who had taken his guilty conscience to the grave with him, and in the absence of any will and testament, they had a right to half our fortune.

Divide it into quarters, one for each of the four of us, they threatened, or the whole thing will come out into the open. It was only with the greatest of difficulty that the wake was prevented from degenerating into a brawl.

Uncle Adolf and Uncle Kurt had lost no time in ensconcing themselves in the upper floors of our house and setting themselves up as so-called financial consultants. After breakfast they consulted the stocks and shares and then made a few calls to the banks. At precisely five o'clock each day, the whole family met either upstairs or downstairs to discuss the measures that had been taken over tea. Uncle Adolf wanted to invest the whole fortune in arms; Uncle Kurt insisted it would be more prudent to spread the risk – as peace seemed to be in the air at the moment – and argued so stubbornly that he finally got his way and invested part of the money in art, where it made an enormous profit. And so it came about that each outbreak of war was greeted loudly by Uncle Adolf, and each declaration of peace by Uncle Kurt. "Peace is for wimps," grumbled Uncle Adolf; while Uncle Kurt raved about all the new museums that had to be built and filled after the War. Thank goodness there were enough wars in the world for Uncle Adolf to make a profit and enough peace-treaties to justify Uncle Kurt's investments. The upshot was that our family did not have to return to work and I was able to go to university.

On my twenty-first birthday – it was raining cats and dogs – I felt that after all the present-giving ceremonies in my mother's rooms, I was at last entitled to ask three questions of the tea-circle: whether my father was alive, what he was called, and why I could not bear his name.

This barrage of questions out of the blue was taken as a sign of my gross ingratitude – for the three of them had secretly been hoping that the only legitimate heir would take his money and keep his mouth shut, but under no circumstances rock the boat.

"Haven't you always been well looked after?" Uncle Adolf demanded, his Adam's apple skipping wildly in his throat.

"If you want war, then on your own head be it," said Uncle Kurt.

"Child, child, how could you do such a thing to your mother?" cried my mother.

My real father, as I went on to establish piece by piece, was called Dietrich von Bluebeard: "a horrifying name for a horrifying man," declared Uncle Kurt. If my mother was to be believed, he had been a terrible womaniser, "but one of those charming, little-boy types," said Uncle Adolf, "whom each woman wanted to mother until he dumped them unceremoniously and went after the next. With his tearful, sensitive disposition and his practised charm he softened up the women," said Uncle Adolf, "until they were like soggy bread rolls, at which point he would find them repulsive and move on to the next victim."

"A mummy's boy, not a man"– was his final judgement. "Our father, your grandfather was the only one not to be dazzled by his noble pedigree: von Bluebeard. If we hadn't come to your mother's aid," said Uncle Kurt, "she would have met with a sorry end."

After a few minutes my mother finally spoke. "Amongst his things we found a locked casket. A golden key that he'd given me on our wedding day fitted the lock and inside we found the marriage certificates of six former wives, with the relevant divorce papers carefully clipped to each one." With that she ran out of the room and brought back a black varnished casket with a golden key in the lock. She spread out all the documents my father had left behind like a fan: all the women my father had loved: Sofie von Arz, Bettine Schwingenstein, Elly Hummel, Corinna Schniewind, Hiltrud Storz and Roswitha von Meyhofer. Last but not least, my mother's marriage certificate, but minus any divorce papers.

"Were you not divorced?" I asked my mother, but got no answer. "Is my father still alive?" I asked Uncle Kurt, who simply shrugged. "Are the other women still alive?" I asked Uncle Adolf. "Who knows," he said vaguely. "I don't think so," replied Uncle Kurt, "otherwise they would have come out of the woodwork by now." "What a dreadful thought," my mother interrupted, "all those women turning up here out of the blue."

There was no more information to be had from the family on the subject of my father: that was clear. All my questions met with excuses about the War and the need to flee amid the general confusion. They claimed there had simply not been time to check what had become of everyone. The three of them seemed determined to preserve their shameful secret for as long as it might prove to be in their best interests to do so, and the more I tried to find out, the more they dug their heels in. The brazenness with which they tried to convince me that they had the upper hand grew less barefaced with each revelation, but there was no doubt that they still had enough to keep me in my place.

Even after my birthday my mother was still unwilling to make common cause with me, her only son and heir, against the pair of scheming uncles, and so I concluded that all three of them must have been involved in the ignominious demise of my father, Dietrich von Bluebeard. Had they killed him? Even if I still hesitated to think that any of my family might belong in prison, as common criminals, this train of thought seemed to be pointing in the right direction. I had to do something to restore my peace of mind — if only to salvage my studies in molecular biology, which had suffered significantly on account of all the family upset.

So I set out alone to track down my father. I convinced myself he would be easiest to find by concentrating on the women. The Munich telephone book turned up a whole list of Schniewinds, which I went through one by one, presenting my father's marriage certificate and enquiring whether any female member of the family had married a von Bluebeard. It was almost too easy, for less than three months later I had discovered the address of a lady now in her eighties. She lived in Goslau, in an old peoples' home, was quite destitute and almost blind, but was ready to receive me without delay to talk about her former husband, my father.

Here is not the place to recount in detail the way Frau

Schniewind, who had in the meantime become the widowed Frau Oehler, was transfigured by romantic infatuation when she began to speak about my father. He was a rogue, a cunning devil, she exclaimed repeatedly, but her dark eyes gazed at me with such a look of adoration that I began to feel quite ill at ease. And his hands and his delicate skin, his manly chest . . . I started to understand why my father had always taken flight. I took my leave when supper arrived, but not without impressing on Frau Oehler, in the presence of the director of the old peoples' home, that she was invited to a magnificent feast to commemorate the memory of von Bluebeard in Munich on Christmas Eve. "You only need call, and I shall fly to you," she whispered to me and pressed my head against her powdered bosom, which smelled of camphor and cinnamon, and would almost have suffocated me if an assistant had not grappled me free.

Less then four weeks later, in June, I had made two further discoveries. In Husum I found Frau Schwingenstein, now Frau Hegenbarth, whose second husband had, as she put it, been lost to the ocean. In Constance I met Frau von Arz who, having divorced my father, had returned to her maiden name and was a passionate mountain-climber, whose efforts on behalf of the endangered flora of the Engadine region had been recognised with the Order of the St Moritz Mountain Rescue Service. Chez Frau Hegenbarth we ate plaice, Frau von Arz preferred partridge, but both of them at once let their food go cold when they began to reminisce about my father and swoon over the man who, to this day and despite everything that had happened, had been the only real man in their lives. A weak man, a hard-boiled fantasist: these were the poles between which the sketchy profile of this man hovered: a man I sought for in vain in my own features. I invited Frau Hegenbarth and her children (two in Hanover and one in Toronto) along with Frau von Arz to the Christmas feast in Munich, and then made myself scarce, as fast as decently possible, as the demands that I stay the night became ever more pressing. "To have a Bluebeard under my roof again," sighed Frau von Arz, with a roll of her eyes, "that would be all I could ever dream of." And with Frau Hegenbarth it was identical.

And Frau Roswitha von Meyhofer, whom I encountered in August in Saarbrücken, also insisted on cataloguing my father's virtues. A charmer, a seducer, she swooned, who, like all charmers, had a bad character, a pig, a sweet cuddly helpless little pig, who liked to think of himself as a Don Juan, repulsive but adorable. I stayed on for dinner and we were joined by three further widows who had all known my father to a greater or lesser degree and represented a fan-club of sorts, which had branches as far afield as Dudweiler and St Ingbert, although my father had only ever spent a year of his life here. All four women promised to come with their families at Christmas in order to honour his memory with his son and heir.

Frau Meyhofer also gave me the address of Frau Storz (now Frau Brandauer) the woman to whom my father had, it seemed still been married when he wed my mother. She neither belonged to the aristocracy nor to the upper classes, as my uncles had claimed. She was pretty in a rather coarse way and unbelievably vulgar. She had married again when my father disappeared and was counted as lost – an advantageous match, as she put it, making the gesture of someone counting their money, but not the best in bed – "not like your father, the old goat," she cackled. "And what I get these days isn't worth talking about," she concluded scornfully before promising to come to Munich at Christmas.

Frau Hummel, whose address had been forwarded to me in November by the detective agency I had taken the precaution of engaging, was no longer quite in her right mind when I visited her in Heidelberg, though she did produce two women whom she claimed were my half-sisters and who drooled over me shamelessly. "You have come back to me at last," she sobbed round my neck. "Here he is again, my lovely boy, my little bear, who lets his mummy tickle under his chin." So now I had tracked down the lot of them: only my father was missing, the restless centre about whom we all revolved.

Shortly before Christmas I had beds made up in all the spare rooms of the house and allayed the suspicions of the family by saying that I wanted to throw a surprise party to celebrate my coming of age. They let me do what I liked, pleased to think that I had been distracted from the altogether more unwelcome search for my real father by my desire for some fun. On 24 December, to the horror of my uncles, the old ladies and their families started to arrive, in even greater numbers than I had anticipated. All of them had brought their photograph albums full of yellowing pictures. Frau von Arz had even dug out my father's dinner jacket, which was then draped over a tailor's dummy that belonged to my mother and took pride of place next to the Christmas tree. Frau Hegenbarth's children brought along a mouth organ and trumpet and provided the musical accompaniment.

On Christmas Eve we were about forty in total, but had one inexhaustible topic of conversation: Bluebeard. My uncles, who had immediately sought refuge in their rooms, were soon hounded out by the women, who had become nothing short of wild, and taken to task so severely that they abandoned all their bank books and savings certificates and could not be seen for dust.

"Ungrateful wretch," whined Uncle Kurt, "we never did you any harm; we even made money for you." "A chip off the old block," yelled Uncle Adolf, waving his fist at the house, whose door he said he would never again darken. After that I was the only man amongst all these women, most of whom stayed on with us after Christmas to help make the most of my father's money – which I had used to set up a special trust fund for just such a purpose.

My mother refused to utter a word. The council which had been elected on the second day and got down to work immediately had decided that she, as the last known wife of Bluebeard, should have a place of honour in our teeming household. She was permitted to sit in Uncle's wing chair, which had been brought down and set up in the middle of the entrance hall, so that she could greet visitors. Behind her there was a screen onto which wedding pictures from each of my father's six weddings were projected on a loop tape – strange images of these ghostly creatures who now scuttled round our house giggling and recounting stories and erotic dalliances from their youth. So when a visitor opened the front door, there sat my mother, decked out in a white dress and a red dressing-gown and all her finery, and glaring vacantly at the new arrival in silence, so that for a moment anyone might have been forgiven for thinking they had stumbled into a madhouse or a film-set. "Is this Bluebeard's house?" The delivery boys would ask several times, but receiving no response from the blank face staring at them, would put down their parcels and scarper.

That spring, we put on a saturnine festival which lasted several days and had been advertised with posters on all the trees and gateposts in the area: Bluebeard's Wedding. The climax of this godless spectacle was that I, standing in for my father, and wearing his dinner jacket and top-hat, would lead each of his brides to the altar. The wedding march was played, flower petals were thrown, a woman dressed up as a vicar would ask whether we would love and honour, forsaking all others, till death us do part. At the very moment when a whispered "yes" departed the lips of the bride, the screen in front of the conservatory would be flung back with a mighty clatter revealing all the other wives who shouted in unison: "No!" thus bringing this blasphemous little show to a close. For the 50 marks we charged for a ticket the audience would get to sit down to a wedding feast at which I presided. It was gruelling and disgusting.

I never learned what my father had really been like, for whenever we began to talk about him – and we did nothing else – the old ladies would roll their eyes and start raving, competing delightedly amongst themselves to come up with the most lewd story. No one will hold it against me when I say that this affected charade which turned exclusively on me, the son of the legendary Bluebeard, began to irritate me to such an extent that one summer's day, as the setting sun bathed our house in a blood-red glow, I decided to disappear without trace and build myself a new life under a false name in a town many miles away. I never married.

The Door

IN OUR HOUSE THERE WAS A DOOR WHICH OPENED ONTO nothing. At first glance it looked like any of the other twelve doors which led, as doors tend to do, to neighbouring rooms or outside. It was stained black, but so that one could see the grain of the wood, finely chiselled maps which illustrated twelve different images of how the world might appear. The door which led to nothing boasted a long and complex creation story, told by a matchstick man who sat just above an almost black knot of wood. My grandfather, who could decipher all twelve wood pictures, loved this door above all the others and when I pushed his chair in front of this one he would trace the lines with his gouty index finger and make them into pictures which he described in detail. I was astonished how the monsters and seas, the sky and its moods, the swelling rivers and the shadowless deserts all came to life under his finger. Sometimes we would simply sit in front of the door in silence for an hour or so, and when my mother – who had a low opinion of Grandfather's fancies – came in and asked what we were doing, he would murmur: "We have just been listening to a story." The only thing that spoiled the look of the door to nothing were the pencil marks that recorded my increasing height.

I remember standing up as straight as I could against the door and having to breathe out so that posterity would not be taken in by my cheating. At some point, though, my mother had given up as I got taller, and the last mark was just above the door-knob. "Why does one stop measuring someone?" I asked my grandfather, and the answer came back straightaway: "Because death begins above the door-knob."

In spite of the many years that he had lived with the door which led to nothing – as a young man my grandfather had built the house himself – it still smelled of wood, of freshly cut wood at sundown. While no one could claim that the wall still smelled of brick, cement or wallpaper, and none of the other wooden furniture in the house – from the table to the oak sideboard – had any scent, the door still gave off a resinous smell that transported you right back to the pine woods on the outskirts of Berlin where the tree, which had furnished wood for our door, had once stood. Next to the door my grandfather had built a small bookcase, where he kept his library dedicated to nothing, almost 300 volumes, as he proclaimed proudly to my classmates lined up in front of it. Some of them were ancient folio volumes, falling to pieces and home to all kinds of little worms and silverfish; the rest were more recent scientific literature stuffed with equations and calculations, in which not even the most meagre living organism would take up residence.

We felt uncomfortable because we could not understand how nothing, of all things, could have generated so many words. The notion that there had been and still were people who dedicated themselves to this alone – hard-baked sophists and sterile researchers who, having dismissed even the most insignificant something as uninteresting, turned to nothing, the dark other of matter – was impossible to fathom. But they existed: that much was clear. To cheer us up our grandfather would sometimes read short stories about nothing, which he had collected over the years in two thick scrapbooks covered in oilcloth. *Nothing Reflected in World Culture* was the title of one book, and set grandfather off on all kinds of tack. A reflection of nothing? But he simply laughed, opened the book and read: "someone once asked Rabbi Ahron what he had learned from his teacher, the great Maggid. 'Absolutely nothing,' he replied. And when people pressed him to explain, he added, 'I learned absolute nothingness, I learned its meaning, I learned that I am absolutely nothing and that I exist nevertheless.'"

"Do you understand?" asked Grandfather, and we nodded, although of course we had no idea how one can be both something and nothing. "You see," he continued, "you just have to heed nothing for long enough and it will reveal itself to you."

As a child I had never had many friends, partly because I was so preoccupied with my family, whose moods and whims took up all my attention and most of my free time, but also because it was frowned upon to bring my school-friends home. "What ugly friends you have," Aunt Hilda would frequently say, "and how unpleasant it is to have them around." She, who according to my friend Thomas was "pig-ugly" herself, with hardly a hair on her head but quite a beard on her chin, made a point of making such comments in front of Thomas, who began coming over less and less frequently until he stopped altogether. To this day I have never been able to bring myself to tell my family that I have been married for ten years, for fear that they might invite my wife for a meal which would be it for once and for all. And of course my wife knows nothing about my family.

It didn't take long before I had no friends whatsoever, leaving my grandfather and his strange obsession as my only companion, unless you count occasional conversations with my parents, which ended, as a rule, unpleasantly. It's either Grandfather or us – at least that is what I understood their strange coldness to mean, and since Grandfather understood something about nothing, while my parents were always going on about education and school reports and good manners, I cast in my lot with my zany grandfather without a second thought. "We two are special, a secret society," he would whisper when we were alone. "Only we know the depths of nothing, the complete absence of being, where everything began and where everything will end." As he said this he would point a quivering finger towards the wooden door in our dining-room, which looked innocent enough and eavesdropped on his conspiratorial tirades impassively.

As long as I could remember, no one had entered the room behind the door. There was no crossing, not even a threshold: just the door. If you peered through the key-hole and felt your eyes getting accustomed to the darkness, you would only see – if you saw anything at all, that is – a thin film of dust moving in the air. There was nothing to see; that much was certain. And when my grandfather asked me what I could see, I would always answer, quite truthfully, "Nothing." He sighed in relief. "For several years now I have been uncertain," he would say, "whether there wasn't perhaps something hiding there after all, a little something, the remains of something else. That would be the death of me."

On one occasion my parents surprised me by coming into the room just as I was peering through the key-hole with my torch. My mother, who had very little sympathy for far-fetched speculation of any kind, gave me a clip round the ear for letting myself get caught up in grandfather's lunacy, but my father knelt down and peered through the key-hole with bated breath. "There really is nothing behind this damned door," he murmured at last. "There never has been anything, and never will be. Nothing, nothing, nothing." As he said it he glared angrily at his father whose lined face looked like a shrivelled apple, as if my father suspected that he knew where the key had been hidden. "You built the house yourself," he hissed through clenched teeth. "You, of all people, must know what is behind the door." "There is nothing behind it," replied my grandfather gently, "really nothing at all."

I cannot really say that the nothing behind the door ever frightened me, as long as my grandfather was alive. When he was taken into hospital – "It's nothing," he whispered as he lay on the stretcher, "I shall be back home before you know it" – I occasionally tried to make some kind of contact with nothing by sitting in front of the door in my arm chair, holding my breath and keeping as still as possible with my eyes closed. I wanted to become part of nothing, a lumpy little addition to this strange phenomenon which was so difficult to grasp. But sooner or later my skin would begin to tingle, my eyelids flickered, or I got pins and needles in my feet. Just at the moment when my body began to dissolve, began to slip weightlessly over into the warm embrace of complete emptiness, and there was nothing else in the way, I would be seized by a sudden fever and shake so violently that I had to get up and return to the world of things. Nothing retreated.

And then came the worst day of my life. We were eating our evening meal, having already watched the evening news, absentmindedly pushing the soggy spaghetti round our plates, when suddenly there was a strange noise. "Behave yourself," said my father, but I hadn't so much as clattered with my spoon. My mother stood up and closed the window to the garden, but before she had sat back down the noise came again: a long drawn-out whimpering sound, which gradually faded away. We three sat at the table in silence and didn't even dare pick up our forks. The third time we realised where it was coming from. It came from nothing. It so clearly emanated from there that there was no doubt about the origin: behind the door leading to nothing there was something trying to communicate with us.

In that moment I knew that my grandfather was dying. So when I finally persuaded my mother to ring the hospital and enquire about him, she learned what I already knew.

Even today, I often think of the door leading to nothing, and of my grandfather, who had built it into his house. He wanted to have something in his house which made coming to terms with the world more difficult. Our knowledge about the world has increased out of all proportion, but we still do not understand the world any better. Quite the opposite. We understand less than ever. He felt that lack. That was why he built the door to nothing in his house, a quite ordinary pine door which, if you got close enough, still smelled of wood, of fresh wood cut at sundown.

The Story of Julius

For Carl, with a C

H E IS CALLED JULIUS AND SITS NEXT TO ME AT SCHOOL. He is very fat; Julius is the fattest kid in the class. No one would say that he is exactly handsome. His ears stick out, Dumbo-ears as we used to say when we were trying to irritate him. He wears glasses with thick lenses. When he took them off you could see his pale eyes and he looked funny.

During class Julius sits quite still with his arms folded and doesn't even move his head when all hell breaks loose. He never puts up his hand up and only says something when he has been asked a question. Not that Julius is stupid.

He always gets "very good" for behaviour, but that's because he never moves. He just sits there and it's an event if he even scratches his mop of red hair with a pencil. "Julius is our very own pasha," the teacher once said, but even that didn't get any kind of reaction.

Julius isn't very popular with the rest of the class and I only sit next to him because there was a spare place at the beginning of the year.

Julius is let off games. When I asked him why he didn't join in with everyone else, he said he found it boring. Then he went and sat down on the touch-line and watched us all, but whether he could see anything through his thick lenses, nobody knew. It was only later that I thought to ask what was more boring, sitting there or joining in, but he had already gone home. I could just make out his bright red hair at the end of the street.

Why was Julius so quiet? Was he unhappy or was he simply shy? I didn't know; nobody seemed to. Perhaps that was the reason that nobody liked him. I had never seen his mother, or his father. I didn't know whether he had any brothers or sisters. When my mother asked me: what is Julius up to these days, the one with the red hair, I would always say that he wasn't up to anything.

Once I invited Julius to my birthday party along with all the others, but the one person who didn't turn up was Julius. "Why didn't you come?" I asked him the next day and Julius said that he was sorry but that he had to do something else.

Why hadn't Julius come? Did he really hate us that much?

I invited him on another occasion and again he didn't come and then said later that he had been ill. Another time he said nothing at all. He peered at me through his thick glasses and didn't say a word.

I told my mother that Julius's mother was seriously ill and that he had to stay at home during the afternoon to look after her. "Quite right," she said, "Julius is a good boy."

One day Julius wasn't at school, and the teacher asked me to go to his house. I was very curious to see what their house was like inside, and straight after school I ran down to the little house at the end of our road and rang the door-bell. Julius opened the door and seemed just like he always did. He certainly wasn't ill. We went into the garden and sat on a bench. Next to Julius sat a fat, black cat, and he was stroking it. That was nice. Fat Julius with the red hair and next to him his fat black cat. It was only on the way home that I realised I had forgotten to ask him why he hadn't been at school.

I told my mother that Julius's mother had died and that he couldn't come to school.

When Julius still didn't come to school the next day I told the teacher that his father was seriously ill and that Julius had to stay at home and help his mother.

I don't remember why I said that. I can still hear myself saying that his father was very ill, and that Julius sent everyone his regards. The others all laughed, as if I had said something funny, and I said you don't laugh about things like that, when someone is ill, and I pretended to be very angry that they were making fun of my friend Julius.

Was Julius my friend?

At break-time the others asked me what Julius's house had been like, what his father did, and whether he had bright red hair too – like Julius. Before I knew it I was telling them one story after another about Julius. I don't know how I thought it all up so quickly. I boasted that Julius's father was a famous explorer who spent most of his time in Africa and had an aeroplane. I made up so many stories so quickly that after a while I couldn't keep track of them at all and one minute Julius was in Africa, the next in a hot-air balloon or in an aeroplane flying over our town. And in Julius's house there were poison-darts hanging on the walls and stuffed crocodiles and in the garden I had seen a lion cub. Really I had wanted to say that Julius had a fat black cat but it came out as Julius has a lion cub in his garden.

Break-time was finally over. As it went on Julius had kept getting bigger and stronger and more exciting, and when I sat down at my desk I noticed that all the others were looking at me because I was Julius's friend, the great Julius.

A fortnight went by before Julius came back to school. He suddenly appeared sitting beside me again – so suddenly that I jumped. There he sat: fat and round, with his red hair, and the sun shining down on the back of his head made his ears all red. Julius sat there in silence with his arms folded. When the teacher asked him how his father was, he said, "Very well, thank you." My heart was in my mouth and I could feel my blood pounding. Suddenly I was terrified of all my lies. But Julius just said calmly "Very well" – and then he was quiet. He didn't even look at me.

But at break-time the fun started. The others came over and wanted to know all about everything. What is it like in Africa? Have you ever shot a lion yourself? What is it like up in an aeroplane, they wanted to know, and what does the school look like from up there? Julius took off his glasses, polished them and then he looked at me and said quietly, "Much the same. Yes," he said, "the school looks much the same from up there." Then he fell silent again.

I was in a terrible state and was relieved when the break was over and classes began again. I wanted to whisper to Julius, but I couldn't, I just couldn't get anything out, my heart was in my mouth.

After school I tried to get away as quickly as I could, but Julius caught up with me and said, "If you like, you can come round this afternoon. My cat has had kittens. Four little kittens," he said again and repeated it once more, but I knew that they weren't lion cubs.

And that was Julius. As soon as he had said it he turned on his heel and walked away with that red hair of his bobbing on the stairs like a flame.

Not long after, Julius and his parents moved away to a different town. Now I sit next to a different boy and sometimes I tell him about my friend Julius.

Else and Sam

M Y GRANDMOTHER'S FAVOURITE PLAY WAS SAMUEL
Beckett's *Krapp's Last Tape*. We had seen it together
in the studio at the Schiller Theatre in Berlin at the end of the
1950s, just when it seemed to me that humanity could be divided
into two separate groups: those who adored Beckett and those
who hated him. Ninety per cent of my school-mates hated him
and thought the Irishman quite mad and so did the teachers at my
school, especially the headmaster, who had earned his professorial
title for achievements in high-jump during the so-called Third
Reich – something that no one who had ever seen him could ever
quite believe. He weighed well over forty stone and had great difficulty crossing a threshold without stumbling. All my aunts hated
Beckett too, along with Chief Post Office Clerk Herr Rehlinger
and his wife, who lived next door and had a poodle called Anton.
I had once had a tortoise who used to roam freely in my garden
with a long leash fastened to his shell, but once when no one
was looking, Anton had bitten off his head – something I could
never forgive. As the dog, like its mistress, had a sweet tooth, I
bought several packets of chewing-gum and squashed them into
a ball, which I then mixed with cream toffees, lured Anton behind

77

the garage and gave him his treat. For three days Anton lay in silence in the garden desperately trying anything he could to get the stuff off his teeth. For three further days he refused to eat, to the consternation of Frau Rehlinger, as he now mistrusted all food. And for all of three years Chief Post Office Clerk Rehlinger refused to speak to me and learned to hate anything that I, now an adult, adored – including Beckett. He even dared to go behind my mother's back to warn my aunts that they should be keeping a closer eye on me to prevent my going off the rails. Although, he sneered, someone who approves of plays in which people sit around in dustbins is probably past saving anyway. At that my aunts hated the Irish writer with a vengeance, as they felt they had a certain interest in my turning out well and indeed hoped to benefit materially in the long term. Moreover the father of a school-friend, Jürgen Herrmann, who in his youth had worked for Siemens in China and had developed a passion for beautiful things, for the exquisite, as he never tired of telling everyone, forbade his son from seeing me, because he was afraid, quite seriously, that I had the power to turn his oaf-ish Jürgen into a Beckett fan.

My grandmother, on the other hand, was completely won over from the start. I can still see us coming home from the theatre huddled together on the top deck of the bus and giggling like besotted teenagers. My grandmother only needed to say, "And the way he took the banana and . . ." for us to laugh like drains, beside ourselves with delight, and happy to have seen something that we knew we would treasure all our lives. The next morning we would continue our conversation at the breakfast-table, much to the disgust of the rest of the family, who felt left out and so tried to make us look silly.

Before the time of our joint Beckett obsession, which lasted three years, I don't think my grandmother can have visited the theatre more than a dozen times. She could recall a production of *A Midsummer Night's Dream* in Leipzig, which she had seen with her father's brother, a famous biologist who had covered her eyes during certain scenes. She had been to the opera in Dresden and to a variety show in Berlin in the 1920s, about which she recalled nothing, save that an actor had come right to the front of the stage and stared directly at her for what seemed like an age – long enough, in any case, to alarm my grandfather. By the time she told me that story my grandfather was long dead, and my mother took to casting doubt on my grandmother's memory.

My grandmother had been a part of my life from the moment I first opened my eyes. That had been during the War in an ivy-covered manor house in a village south-west of Leipzig, in my mother's old bedroom. My father had taken a job which moved him around constantly so that his children were each born in different places all over the world. Only I, the youngest, was lucky enough to see the light of day in my grandmother's own crisp linen sheets. After the end of the War – as my mother had moved to the West to be with her husband and for the sake of my older brothers and sisters – my grandfather, who would never have hurt a fly, was left with just two of the linen sheets, two blankets, two pillows, a wardrobe, a table and three chairs. The rest – the house and its estates, the silver and the Meissen porcelain, the Bohemian glass and the library with its great Bouffon edition with all its original plates, along with all the memories and hopes that had been connected with them – was all confiscated and became the property of the state and people, who had not the faintest idea what to do with most of the windfall and planted crops of second-rate barley and stringy sugar-cane in the remainder. So my grandparents were given a single attic room in the house and estate which had formerly been their own. This room they divided with a screen into two sections, a bedroom and a living-room. And while my grandfather stood day after day in the courtyard that was soon overgrown with weeds, smoking a pipe of home-grown tobacco and shaking his head at the things that were being done, I would crawl into my favourite hiding place and look through the crack between the two beds at the embroidered screen with all its wonderful animals in bright pastel colours, an endless source of my daydreams. My grandfather, this decent and gentle old man, was broken.

During the first few years after the War, when I was a toddler, he would take me with him when he went to the villages to visit his friends and collect food: an egg or a sausage, a thin piece of bacon, some vegetables. But he was soon too weak for these long excursions. After that he would simply sit in his shabby old arm chair, his sunken eyes disappearing even deeper into the folds of his face, his bony arms draped over the chair, so I could see his thick veins, which I would sometimes press to make them disappear for a second. There he would sit, listening with a sigh to the miserable tales I brought back from his former estates.

My grandmother was quite different, and as a life-long Protestant she accepted her fate with complete stoicism. When the pair of them were getting ready for bed behind the screen and I lay on the join between the two beds pretending to be asleep, she would begin her long conversation with God, quite oblivious to grandfather's snoring, which started up almost immediately. First she would say a prayer to get God's attention – after all, he had a good many prayers to listen to at the same time – then she began to address him directly. Although I can't really remember any particular phrases, I do recall the course of the conversation and the general tone. It began with Grandmother reminding the absent deity that he had taken their estates from them. "You have allowed strangers to sit at our table. It was Your will that the beautiful porcelain be smashed. I saw with my own eyes how the parrot on the soup tureen was broken off. And do You find it just that my paintings are hanging in other peoples' rooms? And how can you look on while grandfather sees his machines smashed before his very eyes? And why didn't You intervene when we were being insulted today by the new foreman?" As she could see no reason for this harsh punishment, she would list what she and Grandfather had done for the estates and the people working there. "Did You ever hear a single word against us?" she asked into the darkness. "Did anyone ever have cause for complaint? Did any of the hired hands ever have grievances against us?" But although God was listening – of that I am certain – he did not answer, and so by and by she began indirectly, as it were, to take on his part as well. "It is true, of course, that we dismissed that dairy-man in spring 1939," she conceded, "but You must admit that he was an idler who let his stall go to the dogs. But You can't take away our estates for one little thing like that!" And so it went on, interrupted by little prayers whenever she thought she had gone too far, until she finished by asking God to place his protective hand over her and Grandfather in the future and promised for her part to honour his holy name. And every night she would close by asking God – whatever his plans for me might be – never to turn His love from her grandson. These words always made me almost stop breathing, for fear that I might one day have to deal with God in person. And I would regularly fall asleep worrying about how I would ever recognise him if I met him coming across the fields.

A few years later – my grandfather had died, I had moved to Berlin to be with my family, and Beckett was already famous – Walter Ulbricht finally allowed my grandmother to leave his country. The numerous aunts camping in all the spare beds in our house had managed it, and now it was my grandmother's turn. Ulbricht placed his hopes in the young people of the world, not in old ladies who spoke with a Saxon accent and dreamed of a former time which the Chairman of the Council of Ministers preferred to forget. As she was used to living under the eaves, my grandmother was given an attic room, with her bed, a wardrobe and a little table for her bits and pieces. In pride of place, among these few sorry remnants of her once-great estate, was a pair of curling tongs which she used to curl her hair twice a week with elaborate ceremony in preparation for our twice-weekly theatre visits.

Besides the curling tongs she had four books: the Bible and three novels by Samuel Beckett. To this day I don't know if she had read them.

My mother became increasingly and visibly jealous of our relationship. Sometimes she would even burst into tears when she noticed how close we were. But there was simply nothing better than setting off with my grandmother in her Sunday best – her huge garnet brooch on her white lace blouse – to go and see the weird and wonderful clowns of Samuel Beckett.

When she died I was living in London. Just how painful our closeness must have been for my mother became clear to me when I was not sent a telegram to inform me of her death but a letter, which meant that I missed the funeral. I received the letter on the very day of the funeral, and went into the pub on Camden High Street where Dylan Thomas had wrecked his liver and downed one pint of Guinness after another until closing time. In my drunken stupor I imagined my grandmother like Winnie in *Happy Days* sinking slowly into the ground and disappearing.

A few years later I was in the bar at the Schiller Theatre in Berlin and bumped into Samuel Beckett himself, who was there to rehearse a production of *Godot*. We didn't exchange more than a few words as he was tired after the rehearsal and anyway wasn't a great talker. But our halting conversation did turn to those German writers whom he admired. One of these was Fontane, whose novels he clearly knew well. So I told him that as a girl in Thale in the Harz, my grandmother had sat on Fontane's knee. As I was talking I couldn't resist telling him how much my grandmother had adored his plays in the last years of her life, especially *Krapp's Last Tape* with Walter Franck as Krapp. "That's funny," replied the gaunt man with his lizard face. As our exchange had come to a natural close, I said goodbye and was making to leave when he added: "And give my regards to your grandmother."

My reason for telling this story is, of course, that I still hope that one day my grandmother will be mentioned in the definitive biography of Beckett, in connection with his reception in Germany. If anybody has ever been committed to making him known in Germany, it was she.

My grandmother's name was Else. Sam and Else. To this day I can scarcely imagine a better couple.

The Blue Prince

SOMETIMES AFTER WORK, WHEN I AM TOO EXHAUSTED TO cook, I go to a little place across the road where they still do home cooking. There they serve dumplings with stuffed cabbage, and instead of Hawaii steak with pineapple they do proper roast beef with all the trimmings. The landlady never has to ask what I want; she just brings the special of the day over to the round table where I always sit with the other regulars. Strange people all of them, who seldom speak but are friendly enough towards each other and me, with that sort of old-fashioned courtesy you rarely find in this country of ours.

One day we were joined by a very old lady who didn't seem to be quite right in the head. She kept giving a kind of wink and then opening her battered handbag, which released an unpleasant smell of dust and powder. People called her Your Highness. After some time I offered her a glass of liqueur which she accepted with little grace and then drank down in one. She was staying in a room above the inn, and after the meal the landlord accompanied her to her room with a great show of formality and politeness. As soon as the pair of them had left the room everybody began to speculate wildly about the old lady, and in particular an elderly man whom one could easily have taken for her husband. You often run into that kind of man, usually propping up a bar somewhere, a sort of cross between a con man and a retired sergeant major; they always tell all kinds of stories which are as threadbare as their suits. As the other guests soon went on their way, I ordered another bottle of wine and asked the old dog to tell me the story of the lady who was, we hoped, at that moment sound asleep just above our heads. This he proceeded to do, having first checked that the staff were all busy with clearing up, but in such a rambling and roundabout manner that I didn't dare interrupt, in case he came to a complete halt. People like this have their own rhythm and one just has to accept it as far as possible. He claimed he was an organ-maker from Bohemia who, despite the fact that he was over eighty, was still the one they always called on when the organ and the choir weren't in tune — and he could drink like a forty-year-old, as I discovered the next morning when I went to buy my underground ticket feeling very much the worse for wear. My hangover is also the reason that I would hesitate to stake my life on the accuracy of every word of the story, which I shall now recount as faithfully as I can.

In a region that must have lain somewhere between the Balkans and the Baltic before successive wars changed the face of Europe for ever, there was a kingdom, now long forgotten, that was famous for its good beer, its dry white wine and its first-rate cattle. The bees produced a fine honey which was eaten at the English court, the Romanian king came every year to invigorate his manhood in the warm natural springs, and the fame of the yoghurt, traditionally eaten with blackberries, was such that the neighbouring countries could only be kept at bay with the threat of force. The King had everything he could wish for except an heir. And that was also the reason that his country, that jewel of enlightened monarchy, had begun to fall into ruin. Morale collapses if there are no future generations to look forward to. One can't trust someone without any children. It wasn't long before the whole kingdom was in a parlous state: the beer production dwindled, the wine tasted sour, the cattle did not thrive, the bees flew off never to return and the officials of the court were busy lining their own pockets. Even the stocks and shares plummeted and soon the stock exchanges in Berlin and London suspended trading.

After supper, when the King laid off his ermine stole and went down to the city taverns in disguise to hear what people were saying, his subjects pretended that they didn't recognise him and told him things to his face which pained him deeply. Everyone recognised the King because he had the misfortune to lack a neck: his head sat squarely on his shoulders and he didn't even have an Adam's apple.

"The King doesn't even have a neck," they complained in the taverns. "If he at least had a neck and an Adam's apple, then you could have your photograph taken with him and hang it up behind the bar. But like that? No neck, no Adam's apple, no son and heir; what do we have to be proud of in someone like that?" they asked the King as if he were a stranger, poured him a schnapps and laughed when he disappeared off into the night once more.

The Queen, as befitted her station, was a lady of great elegance. She had met her neck-less husband at the fairground, where she had been selling pancakes with chanterelle mushrooms and a dollop of sour cream. "It was love at first sight," intoned the unctuous Cardinal at their wedding service in the cathedral. And with that all the female subjects had sobbed so piteously that windows all over the country misted over, and the men were moved to chew the tips of their beards. But not very long after the wedding this love went missing somewhere in the echoing corridors of the palace and was nowhere to be found. "You must be patient, my Queen," the Cardinal replied when she made her daily visit for confession but could not think of anything remotely sinful to confess. "Above all you must not contemplate sin, or it will happen of its own accord." So the couple lived their lives, like most couples in their country, politely and remotely, alongside one another.

Every day after breakfast the King sat down on his throne from nine until eleven precisely, with his owl perched on his shoulder and his sceptre in his hand and played at being king. Afterwards he read the newspapers and signed cheques until lunch. The afternoon was spent buried in the library studying how other kings ruled, with brutality and severity, until five o'clock when he would open a playground or drink coffee with a local prince. Then came the masseur who had been instructed to work at massaging him a neck out of nowhere, but every day there was no change to be seen. Then came supper and bed. There was nowhere the King felt so comfortable as tucked up in his own bed. In bed he gobbled down one frivolous book after another, adventure books, dubious novels, political tracts, as he smoked cigars and swigged heavy red wine to make his dreams more exciting. On the occasions that he woke with a start thinking that his people were gathered round his bed laughing at him, he would jump out of bed and wander round the palace in his night-shirt with his hair plastered to his head searching for a place where he could calm his racing thoughts.

One night, distraught and frantic, he ran into the arms of the Queen who had just been celebrating the presentation of the "King's Award for Theatre" in the grand ballroom with the assembled artists of the land, and had been for a walk with the winner in the grounds so that she would at last have something to confess to the Cardinal the next morning. So it wasn't just the wine that made her cheeks flushed and her senses glow. She led the terrified and trembling King into her chamber, turned off the light, slipped out of her clothes and crept into bed next to him, where she comforted the neckless and reckless man who was shivering uncontrollably next to her, until he at last fell asleep.

Nine months later she gave birth to a son. At first he looked much like any other child, with dark hair and a wrinkled face, bent little legs and not a tooth in his head. But after a few years he began to take on the characteristics of royalty – chasing ladies-in-waiting through the castle, charging through the local villages in his carriage pulled by four royal goats in a red livery, setting off rockets in broad daylight, and all in all behaving with such feudal disdain that his subjects thought they must be returning to the Middle Ages. Aged sixteen the Prince threw his first parties which only too often ended in wild and blasphemous orgies, and the King had not even turned fifty when he found himself faced with bevies of girls from the local villages bringing his son's bastard children to lay them on the lowest steps of the throne.

When the Prince turned eighteen the King could stand no more. His wife, the Queen, had stopped going to confession, partly because she couldn't keep track of her misdemeanours, and partly because the Cardinal couldn't tell one sin from another any longer. In the absence of any moral guidance, she simply sank deeper into the bottomless morass of debauchery and the King realised that if anyone was to take charge of their son, it had to be him.

He tried to teach him the rudiments of economics and gave him lessons in marketing, statistics and other business skills, which were intended to put him in a position to steer the kingdom in a responsible fashion when he was older. The King even curtailed his newspaper-reading and restricted his throne-sitting to only half an hour per day and coffee-drinking with princes to twice a week, in order to have time for the young man who, for his part, made no great effort to digest the material. Indeed he showed so little interest in business and statistics or economics and marketing that the King began to fear for the future of his kingdom and his royal wealth. Not very long afterwards, the Prince started drinking. If one could turn a blind eye to the beer at breakfast, the Burgundy at lunchtime was more difficult to ignore and the glasses of schnapps all afternoon, while the Prince was doing his sums, left the King beside himself with fury. Not infrequently the King had to summon one of his servants to help haul the drunken Prince to his bedroom, where surrounded by his crowd of dissolute women and their brats he would sleep it off snoring loudly. The first thing he did on waking was to reach for the bottle to see off his throbbing head, but it was not unknown for him to take an accidental slug from the bottle of Cologne next to the bed.

The country went downhill along with the Prince. The hops rotted on the trellises, the wheat hung limply in the fields and the cattle lay around listlessly in the fields, as if they were taking a lead from their masters. The citizens sat tight-lipped and grim in the taverns drinking away their last money and when the King timidly put his head around the door to ask whether his son had been there, they showed no respect for their monarch. "You should take a look in the Golden Stag," they said in the White Hart. "He was in the Black Boar a moment ago," growled the landlord of the Pigalle in his filthy shirt.

One day the King finally snapped. He no longer wanted to be King. He called his subjects to him, put on his crown, seated himself on the throne and then, before his assembled court, citizens and a delegation of princes, he announced his abdication and the end of the royal house. With that he shooed the owl from his shoulder, flung the sceptre into the lap of his babbling son, gave the Queen's lover – a second-rate actor who was struggling to retain his composure – a hefty clip round the ear, packed up his crown in a bag with the royal casket and a few bank certificates, and marched past the astonished assembly – upon whom it was dawning, all too slowly, that much worse times were round the corner – and out into the castle courtyard where a carriage pulled by six horses met and him and bore him, without further incident, out of his country and far away.

He never returned to his kingdom. Years later his people, who now laboured under the merciless yoke of unscrupulous bureaucrats, learned that he had settled in Cairo and won the heart of an Italian soprano who had given him a daughter – if such a thing is permissible for a man over seventy.

On his death-bed he made this daughter, Paola, promise that she would one day return to his kingdom to find out whether anyone still remembered him. "Even when I am no longer of this world," he murmured, and gazed up at that realm where he would be welcomed only as a citizen, "it would comfort me to know that I am remembered fondly." Paola, who attended the English School in Cairo, was used to every second class-mate claiming to be descended from south-east European nobility. But that her father, whom she had always known and loved as a quiet, unassuming man who sometimes played the impresario for her illustrious mother, should suddenly indulge in such incredible and high-flown fantasies was not to her taste.

"Where is the country I should visit? What is the country called where you were once King?" she asked her dying father, whose sombre reveries made him seem strange to her. But there was no answer. With his last strength the old man pointed with one bony finger under the Arabian four-poster bed, where a scruffy bag could be seen, and then his body gave up its last. His daughter got quite a shock when she reached into the bag and pulled out a splendid crown, a sheaf of bonds, and any number of expensive jewelled trinkets. A week later, when her mother had returned from Dresden at the end of her tour, and her father had been laid to rest in the peaceful Egyptian soil, the two women, who had been completely in the dark until then, decided that after her exams the girl should journey to the distant land whose name she had discovered from the documents in the bag and carry out her father's last will.

No sooner said than done. But not very far beyond the border that separated that distant country from its richer and more civilised neighbours, as the elegant young lady in her finest English tweeds settled down for her first night in a local tavern, she was set upon and mugged. This meant that she would have to endure a long wait while the money for which she had telegraphed home was sent. The tavern was packed with a rough crowd: some of them turned up first thing in the morning, others stayed overnight, but clearly none of them had anywhere else to go. They drank beer first thing, sour wine at lunchtime and then switched to schnapps and water until the small hours. All day they swayed and staggered, jostled and spat, and since these foul and bedraggled creatures spoke none of the languages taught at the English School in Cairo there was no chance of any civilised exchange with any of them. There was one who would sometimes seem to come to after a period of vacant staring and begin to babble in strange tongues – although a civilised person would have great difficulty in construing a French sentence out of the incoherent scraps. Nevertheless it was a comprehensible language and the fact that it only seemed designed to keep up the steady flow of alcohol did not deter the young woman from trying to make contact with this miserable fellow. He exuded an acrid stink of goats and sheep and when he opened his mouth one had to keep one's distance to stay standing at all. "I am the daughter of the King," she cried desperately through the haze of alcohol fumes and in the general direction of the drunken wretch, who left her in no doubt of his response. "And I am his son!" he slavered. "A schnapps for the children of the King!"

It did not take long for the determined young woman to establish at the local Prefecture that this bloated creature was indeed the son of the last King, that admired monarch who had then abandoned his kingdom and left his people to wrack and ruin. He had, she learned from a bureaucrat who fixed his watery eye on her bare knee, made off to Cairo and squandered the royal coffers with a dubious chanteuse. "Since he disappeared," the man sighed, "this country has gone to the dogs, and when the last reserves have been eaten, the last wine drunk, then our poor country too will disappear under the merciful veil of oblivion. The Blue Prince" – the name given to the stinking drunkard – "will extinguish the memory of our noble history for ever."

The rest of the story can be told briefly enough. While the young woman was still waiting at the tavern for her money to arrive, the World War broke out and changed the face of Europe with its barbaric ferocity. The curious pair began an itinerant life together, settling in Agram and then in Paris, where the Blue Prince drowned himself in absinthe. His sister never married, although she spent a number of years during the War as the companion of a Russian aristocrat and gambler in Nice. The Princess never saw her mother again although she still has a shellac record with a recording of her voice. The crown went under the hammer at an auction house in New York during the early 1970s when an Egyptian wool-merchant put it up for sale; the buyer wished to remain anonymous.

"And that is the whole story," said the garrulous old man at last, and with that he downed the last of the fourth bottle of wine, waved at the staff, who lay huddled in a corner on the bench, with a regal gesture, pressed his shabby straw hat onto his head and tottered out of the tavern.

"But who are you?" I called after him as he disappeared, as a sudden idea had begun to form in my foggy brain, but there was no reply. When I finally made my way out into the night I gazed up drunkenly at the façade of the Wilhelmine house which arched over the little inn. In her room Her Highness's light was still burning.

Moon Enterprises Inc.

WHEN GRANDFATHER ARRIVED, THE WEATHER CHANGED, and so did our life at home. Whereas we had always gone about our everyday business as a matter of course, and come together at lunch and over supper to talk it over, now everything began to revolve around my grandfather. In our family Grandfather was the sun and we were the planets whose only light came from him and who could do nothing but revolve around him.

He looked as if he had been cut out of paper and slept in the living-room, but because he snored with a sound like rustling paper, Uncle Herbert, who lived in the drawing-room next door, was forced to sleep in the kitchen on a sofa. Uncle Herbert was a writer and worked at night, so that every morning my mother and sisters would haul him out of the smoky kitchen and drag him into the dining-room, where he could doze on the dining-room table until lunchtime. On the far side of the living-room was a kind of over-size larder which was home to two of our aunts. No one knew how they were related to us. Aunt Number One and Aunt Number Two had come to live with us from the East, nobody knew when, and had stayed, much to the consternation of Uncle Herbert, who had been with us even longer and deemed the pair of them unliterary. Uncle Herbert never read anything either, but at least he actually owned books, although what he wrote in the drawing-room at night when Grandfather wasn't there was anybody's guess. "Is your book out yet?" Grandfather would growl at him the minute he sat down in his arm chair, and Uncle Herbert would lower his eyes in the face of such barbarous behaviour. Aunt Number Two, who was never allowed to open her mouth in Grandfather's presence because she spoke with a strong Saxon accent, would giggle, my two sisters would glare sternly, and only my mother who had some kind of heartfelt faith in Uncle's scribbles said cheerfully, "If it becomes a best-seller we will all go on holiday to Italy," though not even that was enough to save my uncle.

My father never said a word.

My grandfather had dedicated his life to the moon. If a war broke out anywhere in the world he would consult his charts and say, "It was written in the stars." When a war came to an end, it was the result of the moon's influence; if Aunt Number One dropped a plate, an almost daily occurrence, he would raise his papery finger and point to the ceiling in the direction where the moon might be. And when Mother insisted that Aunt Number One should pull herself together, he would snigger gleefully to himself. She could pull herself together all she liked; it was the moon that sent the plate flying. My father had amounted to nothing, according to Grandfather, because he was born at a full moon; Grandmother's unfortunate encounter with oncoming traffic had happened because she crossed the road on the third day of the waning moon; my sisters would never marry because they had been conceived at a moment of libration; Uncle Herbert was a lunatic, that went without saying; and as for the aunts, he dared not even begin for fear of offending the moon. "How on earth could you ever have married a man born under the full moon?" he demanded of my mother. "A dreamer and a fool?" And at the dinner table he would ask me out loud how I could stay with this motley moon brood. "Run away; get out of here: find yourself a better constellation," he said with his rustling voice. "In this house you will come to a sorry end."

Because I had come into the world a few days later than predicted, I had just succeeded in manoeuvring myself into a favourable phase of the moon, according to my grandfather. "If things had gone the way your parents intended," he would often say at table, "you would have been a complete moon-calf. Your precocious intelligence saved you; let's hope it can save you from your family too." When Grandfather was visiting, he was the only one to speak, and I kept quiet too, as my school results had nothing of the waxing moon about them. Only Aunt Number Two, who, if truth be told, lived altogether beyond the moon, would giggle to herself. "Don't take him too seriously," my father would say, when Grandfather had finally taken his leave and we could sit in the living-room again watching television. But the very mention of the moon in a weather forecast brought him back and Grandfather would be sitting there with us again. Floods, heat-waves, coups and deaths – they were all naturally caused by the moon. If the Left were victorious anywhere in the world, they had shamelessly fixed the vote for a particularly auspicious Monday and if the Right won, they had been canny enough to pick this day and this alone for voting. That was the way it was, it was all ordained – that was our unanimous opinion – and there was nothing to be done this way or that. Even Uncle Herbert, who hated the television, because he didn't like the way the announcers spoke and because he reckoned the weatherman was trying to ingratiate himself with him – something my mother thought a touch over-sensitive – even Uncle Herbert would sometimes grudgingly admit that the moon had a hand in things.

And so we sat evening upon evening with our moon-charts in front of the TV and passed comment on the affairs of the world. Aunt One giggled, Aunt Two fumbled her way through diagrams of planetary orbits, my mother sighed when the moon began to wane, my sisters had given up looking for husbands and fell in love with the newscaster, my father had a suspicion that business would go badly, Uncle Herbert found fault with the announcer's unbearable lisping, and it fell to me to consult the tables to discover what disasters would befall us the next day.

As summer drew to a close, Grandfather turned up again and the weather changed. That was all that happened, but that was catastrophic enough. "It cannot go on like this," said Grandfather, who now looked like paper that had been shredded and screwed up. This time, along with his moon-tables, he had brought a telescope too, in order to scrutinise this harbinger of good and ill more closely. "That is godless behaviour," my mother said, but didn't do anything, even when the builders came and bored a hole in the living-room ceiling so that Grandfather could observe the moon from his arm chair through the attic-window in my bedroom. But since the moon did not stand still, a second hole had to be made, and my parents immediately took to separate beds so that the telescope could be trained on the moon between them. At the end of the year, when the clear nights began, our house, with its six glazed portholes for moon-watching, looked like a modernist cheese – and Grandfather was the maggot in the middle.

Our family life had changed overnight. The expense of rebuilding our house had forced Father to sell his business, something which pleased Grandfather no end, as he now had an assistant for the night vigils, who could catch up on sleep all day. The sisters and aunts were decamped to the cellar, where they were given quite attractive dungeon-quarters, which they partitioned with screens. After much complaining, vents for light and air were added so that their cellar-life became rather comfortable. Sometimes I saw them creeping through the house with their wan faces, and sometimes you could hear the Saxon giggle of Aunt Number Two drifting up from the cellar steps.

My mother went shopping just before the shops closed so that the moon-watchers got their food promptly at midnight. She got back in time for the evening news and the weather, and that was the signal to get up. For the whole of that winter, the majority of our house never saw daylight. At about seven in the morning Grandfather and Father drank a last little schnapps, sometimes even with Uncle Herbert, who had just finished his night's work and made his way to his sofa in the kitchen.

I was the only one who had a daytime routine that bore any resemblance to the rest of the population. As the family were preparing to go to bed in the morning, I was getting up to go to school. When I got back, someone would sometimes appear in the kitchen in pyjamas to get a glass of water, or a voice from the cellar would ask what time it was, as night and day were indistinguishable down there. Aunt Number One started sprouting hairs on her chin and looked more and more like a potato, beginning to sprout in the cellar. Aunt Number Two developed rheumatism and spent all her time in bed. And as for the sisters, who had let themselves go a bit and begun neglecting their clothes and appearance, once they had got a video there was no stopping them. They were glued to it, day and night, comparing the weather forecasts with the ones from the previous week and the previous month and hardly ever ventured out above ground.

Father's appearance was heartrending: pale, with bloodshot eyes, he sat up when I woke him in the evening but never uttered a word of complaint. It was the moon's will: pointless to try and rebel against this life. Grandfather was in his element at last: all his instruments gathered around him, he sat wrapped up in blankets in his arm chair and directed the operation. The results were all entered in huge folio volumes and sketched onto the astronomical charts that covered every wall of our house. And scarcely two years later – presidents had come and gone; governments had been toppled; famines had killed thousands of people – Grandfather announced that he had discovered the secret of the moon. But this discovery brought the beginning of the end for my family; and as the last surviving member, I had to see it through all its phases.

The tragedy – to cut a long story short – was that Grandfather, in order to save the world, wanted to sell his knowledge. Loans were secured; the house was altered again, fax-machines were installed, along with computers and a small printing-press, and the four women were released from the cellar and trained up so that they could produce the moon news updates and distribute them. Governments were briefed, banks were informed of imminent crises, and famines were predicted. Aunt Number One was in charge of divorces, Aunt Number Two furnished long-range forecasts for the agricultural industry; the sisters kept in contact with all the foreign embassies, my father manned the computer, mother cooked, Uncle Herbert was employed as a secretary and directed the moon news, and in May I passed my A-levels.

In June the trial began. It ended in September – every detail predicted correctly by Grandfather – with a guilty verdict. Our firm, Moon Enterprises, had plagued the world with predictions – had known that half the world would divorce; that some people would die of hunger, while others would be killed in car accidents; and others again would jump out of windows – but no one wanted to know it, or at least no one wanted to pay for the information. The family was forbidden from concerning itself with the moon any further; the instruments had to be sold to pay the creditors and the house went under the hammer. Not long after, Grandfather died. He put his final energies into lasting just a few days longer so that he could enter a favourable phase of the waxing moon, but didn't manage it. He died on a dark night when the moon was hidden from view behind a thick bank of cloud.

Murder Most Ordinary

TODAY ON 20 SEPTEMBER 1993, THE 49-YEAR-OLD editor, Christopher Horschick, of 149 Luisenstrasse, 80333 Munich, entered the police station in Starnberg and made the following statement:

I, Christopher Horschick, have been editor in charge of the literary work of the writer Klaus C. Schulz at the publisher C.H. König and Sons for twenty years: 12 novels, 4 volumes of prose poetry, 2 collections of poetry, 4 editions of drama, 2 volumes of critical works, speeches and collected writings: all in all, 24 volumes with 8,000 pages.

During the course of those twenty years Herr Schulz has received every West German literary prize of any importance – the most significant being the Bavarian Literary Prize, the Lower Bavarian Cultural Prize, the Prize of Upper Bavaria, the Golden Pen of the Freising Literary Friends, and the Honorary Medal of the Artists' Social Security Fund, but also the Bürger-, Holty-, Wackenroder- and Uhland-Prize, the Helgoland Bursary, and the Honorary Grant of the Cultural Circle of the Franconian Business Guild – in total about 240,000 marks.

My job as an editor (net salary to date 4,150 marks per month) consisted of being a kind of universal minder for the person and work of Herr Schulz, who as the child of Swabians from the Banat, only discovered his writerly calling after moving to West Germany. He finished work on his debut novel, *What the East Wind Tells Us*, published in Munich in 1973 (16th edition in 1992), in my apartment at 64 Herzogstrasse, because he didn't have the money for a place of his own, and the rest of his work came into being in the Starnberg Villa, which after twelve years of paying rent finally became his.

Since Herr Schulz's knowledge of punctuation was rudimentary, 70 per cent of his commas, exclamation marks, and his characteristic semi-colons were (insofar as they appeared in the correct places) my own. Moreover, the titles of the majority of his books resulted from my suggestions, in particular, the title of his best-seller, *The Hare Conspiracy*, which was later to become a film – and would, if Herr Schulz had had his way, have been called *In Thrall to Innocence*. Almost all the proper names which appear in his novels, from the now legendary "Red Roswitha" in *For Whom the Heart Beats*, to "Stuttering Dieter" in *Beyond the Hills*, are my inventions, and even "Old Father Schlupp", who appears in every Bavarian sixth-form textbook with his rambling anecdotes, got his name from me. The opening lines of every novel and the closing ones of 90 per cent of them are the result of my endeavours, for, as Herr Schulz has often confirmed, he never knows how to begin a story or end it. Even Herr Schulz's reputation for eloquence, which has rightly garnered so much praise, owes a good deal to my intervention. It was I, for example, who took the endlessly repeated "he said" and made of it a whole gamut of new possibilities: "he remarked", "he averred with a growl", "he mentioned, as if in passing", "he murmured into his bushy beard". That I simply corrected the manuscript when the hero, who a few pages before had been residing in a villa, was suddenly slumming it in a two-bedroom flat, goes without saying.

But even if one can reckon such minor embellishments and corrections to be part of the normal task of the editor, then the same cannot be said of my contribution to Herr Schulz's lyric output. I wish it to be recorded before witnesses that the poems in the collection *Breathed onto Water*, for which Herr Schulz, and not the real author, received the Bavarian Giro and Savings Bank Prize (30,000 marks) were almost entirely my own creation along with the title poem, 40 pages long, which Professor Zink von Giessen, in his *Laudatio*, set alongside poems by Hölderlin and other literary greats. The manuscripts and proofs that have remained in my possession prove without any shadow of a doubt that, aside from the formulation "in the chalky twilight of autumn", Herr Schulz's contribution amounted to exactly zero. In response to my written proposal that Klaus C. Schulz might care to dedicate at least one of "his" poems to me, I was informed by telephone that it would be unique in literary history for an author to dedicate his own work to himself. And so my name does not appear anywhere in the book.

After that it came as no surprise when Herr Schulz asked me to draft his acceptance speech for the prize, which he then declaimed word for word in the foyer of Schwabing Savings Bank to thunderous applause, and which is still considered today as his most important poetological statement and is quoted and reproduced in every doctoral dissertation written about his work: "Is poetry anything more than the ceaseless attempt to breathe words onto water?" – you recognise it of course.

In short, I would like to suggest, in all modesty, that the work of Herr Schulz – honoured with so many prizes, translated into so many languages, and known in every corner of Germany – would not exist without my contribution – a fact which Herr Schulz, after scarcely more than a bottle of his specially named vintage wine, has always been prepared to concede ("where would I be without you, my dear Horschick!"), but once sober denies any memory of.

Six years ago, on the way home after the presentation of the Robert Neumann Medal (in my car!) – after I had given the *Laudatio*, and he had given the speech of thanks I had written for him – I suggested for the first time that in future we should split any prize-money 70:30. Four years ago I threatened not to work on his novel *The Old Song* if I had no share in the profits, but then allowed myself to be persuaded by my literary conscience to save the manuscript after all (for which, incidentally, under the title *The Scream*, and with a completely new central character, set in a different century and furnished with a new story-line, he collected the prize for the best foreign novel in Paris). Three years ago I refused to work his prose poetry up into a libretto, with the result that the piece was a disaster, a spectacular flop, and brought his most bitter recriminations. Two years ago, on completion of the four-part television adaptation of *With All Good Wishes*, he gave me, instead of the 40,000 marks I had asked for, his old television set; and last year, to cap it all, when I asked him for a temporary loan against monies owing to me, so that I could take my new companion to Paris on holiday, he sent me 200 marks with a note "Have a good meal on me". Now, this spring, after the run-away success of his novel *The Women of Ambach* (my title), I suggested that he appoint me as editor of the projected special edition of his *Complete Works* which was to mark his seventieth birthday and give me a 2 per cent share of the royalties – an equitable sum, or so I reckoned, in recompense for my work over the years. His reaction was depressing.

My final attempt to find some way of connecting my name – which appeared nowhere in the 8,000 pages of Herr Schulz's oeuvre, not as a dedication, acknowledgement, not even in a footnote – with the work I had written was to try and reach an amicable agreement. As Herr Schulz had no heirs apart from his former wife (to whom I had introduced him in the first place) I proposed that he should make the rights to his work over to me in the case of his death. This last suggestion was greeted with the retort: "Over my dead body!" And so this morning I bought myself a ticket to Starnberg, entered Herr Schulz's study from the terrace, took the bronze bust of Ludwig Uhland out of his special cupboard, and struck him several times with all my strength on the back of his head, until I could be sure that I would never have to read or edit another line of his in my life.

Starnberg, 20 September 1993
Signed C. Horschick

Police Superintendent Koch and the undersigned immediately

repaired to the house of the writer by the name of Schulz in order to ascertain the truth of the above statement regarding the corpse, which was indeed discovered at 14.30 hours in a lifeless condition, whereupon the editor Horschick was taken into custody.

Starnberg, 20 September 1993
Signed: P.J.W. Jobst

Epilogue

Alcohol and Literature

EVERY WRITER DRINKS. WHAT CAN NOT PERHAPS BE gleaned from their simple writers' graves is, however, revealed if one studies their non-canonical works – letters and diaries, for example: world literature lies under a fog of alcohol. Some find it a matter of great concern that the greatest works of literature owe their existence to alcohol; for others it is a source of comfort. That strange man who has spent the last thirty years on the sofa hugging a beer-bottle might be an unrecognised genius, after all. Goethe's wine-consumption has been recorded down to the tiniest detail; that you could smell the alcohol on E.T.A. Hoffmann's breath at ten paces is well-documented; the fact that the Great American Novel, from Hemingway to Faulkner, emerged from the bottom of a whisky glass is no secret; even the great German literature of the present, from Joseph Roth (the miserable drunkard) to Uwe Johnson, is unthinkable without alcohol. It was the Nobel Laureate Joseph Brodsky who used to say that "ninety per cent of the best lyric poetry is written *post coitum*". Today we know that – before, during and after – alcohol is the key.

Our century, with its insatiable thirst for knowledge, has set itself the task of shedding light on the dark complicity between wine and literature, the fluid boundaries between the intoxication of reading and the delights of drunkenness. It has professed itself less than satisfied with the assertion that a writer on the bottle only has to open his mouth for perfect prose to pour forth, whereas a teetotaller chews over his words obsessively until he can't get a single one out. It is no longer enough to say that writers of a Dionysiac bent drink. They have to drink. They reach for the bottle more often than they reach for a pen, and whereas their fluency may increase with wine their productivity certainly does not.

In this age of measurements and of statistics – a device that was originally invented for purposes of surveillance – it was not enough to distinguish exactly where literary truth becomes drunken fiction and vice versa, but rather to establish whether there are parallels to be drawn with the drinking habits of ordinary readers. In short: What precisely is the correlation between reading and drinking?

Here I would like to present the results of my research to date and take this opportunity to set down my conclusion straight away. Societies that are committed to truth to the exclusion of all else have an unhealthy relationship to alcohol; societies that rely on literature to an excessive degree have an unhealthy relationship to truth; and societies that are entirely dependent on alcohol have an extremely unhealthy relationship to both truth and literature. But statistics would not be statistics if exactly the opposite had not also been proven to be true. There are, for example, populations of alcoholics who are extremely receptive to truth and literature, lovers of literature who are nevertheless devoted to truth, and disciples of truth who are permanently off their heads. It is the subtle gradations that are significant here.

Wolfgang Rihm, in his definitive survey, *Alcohol and German Studies* (Paderborn, 1978), concludes that the following three statements meet with the greatest approval among literary scholars.

1. Alcohol has the effect of making one feel comfortable, even in the company of writers.
2. Alcohol facilitates contact with people who have never read a book.
3. Alcohol can even make a Professor of German appear imaginative and witty.

On the other hand, the "Foundation for Reading", financed by Bertelsmann among others, correlated results from 700 representative German professors from a range of disciplines and discovered that intensive consumption of books and alcohol produced the following effects:

1. that one felt uncomfortable in the presence of writers;
2. that contact with students who had never read a book decreased or broke down completely;
3. that the subjects of the study never managed to appear humorous, imaginative or witty.

If we set these two sets of statements alongside one another, we are bound to come to the conclusion that a greater readiness among literary critics to consume alcohol goes hand-in-hand with increased sociability. Moderation is all-important, however. For it stands to reason that those literary critics who are heavy drinkers and have never finished a book in their lives are socially beyond the pale – although, as we know only too well, the number in this category is increasing daily. Whereas literary critics who read a great deal but never touch a drop are, thank goodness, still a minority.

Some light is shed on the causes if we compare the pro rata consumption of wine in Western Europe. Statistics from 1977 indicate that the Germans – before German unification that is – drank 23.4 litres of wine a year; the Irish only 4.3 litres, the Spanish 65 litres, the Italians 93.5 litres and the French 100.9 litres. If we compare the pro rata book consumption the picture becomes clearer:

Germany	23.4 litres of wine =	20 books per year
Ireland	4.3 litres of wine =	4 books per year
Spain	65 litres of wine =	4 books per year
Italy	93.5 litres of wine =	6 books per year
France	100.9 litres of wine =	12 books per year

The statistics demonstrate beyond any shadow of doubt that, as far as wine is concerned, Germany and Ireland achieve a balanced ratio: 23.4 litres of wine are required for the reading of 20 books (West Germany) and 4.3 litres for 4 books (Ireland). Set against that the 100.9 litres required in France for a measly 12 books. There is no need, I think, to spell out the disastrous economic implications any further.

On the production side, granted, the picture looks rather

different. According to Pittmann / Schneider (Wolfenbüttel, 1982) a German professor requires approximately 18 litres of wine to complete a philosophical manuscript of approximately 360 pages – that means 0.05 litres, or one mouthful, per page; whereas a French philosopher requires all of 24 litres for a 30 page essay on ethics – i.e. a bottle of wine per page. I do not believe I need to elaborate here on the causes of the relative dryness of German philosophy.

Now you will object – and rightly so – that a German philosopher does not only drink wine when he is writing his major works, but beer and schnapps too. And indeed the World Health Organisation figures (Rome, 1987) tell a quite different story. According to the WHO, the pro rata consumption of 100 per cent proof ethanol in Western Europe is as follows:

Germany	15.8 litres	=	20 books
Ireland	12.6 litres	=	4 books
Spain	19.3 litres	=	4 books
Italy	16.8 litres	=	6 books
France	21.3 litres	=	12 books

You will notice that it is heavily weighted towards consumption. A Spaniard has to consume nearly 20 litres of pure alcohol in order to read all of four books: that is 5 litres per book. And when you consider that the greatest works of Spanish literature are all slim volumes of poetry, then you will appreciate what an uphill struggle it is for the Spanish publishers' association to reduce the levels of alcohol tolerance to a point where they can sell a book at all. Germans require 0.8 litres per book, the French 1.7 litres, the

Italians almost 3. I don't believe it is an insult to say that Italians clearly prefer drinking to reading.

One final set of figures. The German Writers' Union has published the following statistics for its various branches.

	Beer	Wine	Spirits		Total in Litres
Dramatists	190	140	7.5	=	337.5
Poets	40	260	12.4	=	312.4
Novelists/					
Essayists	240	180	16.5	=	436.5
Critics	60	50	6	=	116
Total	530	630	42.4	=	1,202.4

If, for amusement's sake, one adds up the total alcohol consumption of all the writers in the German Writers Union and divides that total by the number of pages produced by those same authors, one comes to a final figure – contrast the philosophers on 0.05 litres of wine per page (see above) – of 1 litre of wine, 3/4 litre of beer and a double measure of spirits per page, which, if one considers that a standard novel has about 300 pages, represents a significant expenditure, one rarely offset by royalties.

If, on the other hand, one compares these figures with the alcohol consumption of the average reader, an even more shocking picture emerges. While a German writer, as has been established, consumes 1 litre of wine, 3/4 litre of beer and a double, the reader, according to Heinemann / Reuband (Göttingen and New York, 1984) needs 1.6 litres of wine, 2 litres of beer and a treble in order to swallow a single page of German prose. All of which raises the issue of who is at fault – if a notion like fault has any place here – the writers or the readers?

But enough statistics. We all know that statistics can lie. When in a recent survey German authors were asked which letter came after A, only 40 per cent would commit themselves to B, and 18 per cent not at all, and in a survey of wine-merchants 24 per cent claimed never to have come into contact with alcohol. We are familiar with this kind of thing.

Nevertheless there are a number of conclusions that can be drawn. The search for a balanced relationship between consumption of alcohol and literature in EU countries should at least take account of the following considerations:

1. The simultaneous and equal availability of alcohol and literature in book shops, libraries, and universities.
2. The most extensive possible distribution of literature and wine – staggered according to age, gender and percentage of drinking population.
3. The formalisation of drinking and/or reading rituals: time, place and manner of ingestion (down in one, page-skimming, etc.).
4. The frequency of consumption of alcohol and/or literature: daily, weekly, monthly.
5. The duration and extent of reading and/or drinking.
6. Context of literary and/or alcoholic consumption: During a religious service? During a party? With a meal? Covert reading/drinking in an identified subgroup? Reading/drinking alone?
7. Behavioural traits attendant on said reading/drinking:

antisocial inclinations, boasting, exhibitionism, hostility, vomiting, black-outs, feelings of guilt or superiority: "I can do more novels than you", etc.

8. Attitude to uncontrolled reading/drinking: denial, approval, citing diminished responsibility as a defence: "I have read too many poems/drunk too much wine".

9. Problems which emerge as a result of excessive alcohol/literary consumption: health problems, economic, social, moral, etc.

Once these aspects have been fully correlated, a certain consensus will be established and three general conclusions will emerge:

1. Wherever alcohol and literature are known, rules will be developed for their enjoyment: reading and drinking in groups, or alone. Reading and drinking out of despair, etc.

2. If a culture develops gender-specific restrictions on reading or alcohol consumption, it is normally women who have restricted access to drink and men who have restricted access to books (Hartwig, 1980).

3. A change in economic conditions, social structures or in the material culture causes a change in drinking or reading habits. Consider East Germany before and after the events of 1989, for example. Whereas before 1989 excessive book-reading was both a documented habit and an officially approved aim, now there is nothing but aimless boozing. Or take Bavaria: during those periods when strong beer comes on tap for the first time the consumption of

lyric poetry goes down by 68 per cent (Lower Bavaria) or 72 per cent (Franconia). Given that poetry-reading in Bavaria anyway represents only 14 per cent of reading in total, measured against Germany as a whole, it is clear that Bavarians read only two or three lines of poetry per month during the beer season: Jandl perhaps:

> ottos dogs gone
> otto: ogogogod

In conclusion, a few points attempting to explain the fact that in some EU countries people seem to drink excessively while in others they read just as excessively.

1. The Angst hypothesis
   The primary function of novels and the accompanying drop in drinking levels is the reduction of Angst (Härtling, 1964): "I have read the new Günter Grass, nothing can touch me now."
2. The social disorganisation hypothesis
   According to this hypothesis, excessive, "intoxicated" consumption of literature occurs in cultures which operate with minimal levels of political organisation, and without complex social hierarchies or comparable institutions. In such socially undifferentiated societies there are few mechanisms for controlling informal, aggressive or poorly-structured reading habits. The result: minimal drama (often one-act plays) and substantial novels.
3. The ethno-psychological conflict dependence hypothesis
   According to this hypothesis, conflicts around issues of

independence and self-esteem which have their roots in an inconsistently administered system of reward during childhood can be the catalyst for:

(a) an excessively heavy reading programme (Bayer gives the example of an eighteen-year-old who read Fontane's *Complete Works* in 6 weeks) which in turn leads to

(b) excessive drinking.

Finally:

4. The impotence hypothesis

Wagenbach (1960) claims that excessive reading is generally to be found in communities where economic instability determines social hierarchies. Reading, according to him, gives readers the feeling that they are powerful and in control. If, however, they become aware that these feelings are illusory, they abandon the book and turn to the bottle. Consider, for example, the sequence of events that Wagenbach (pp.312 ff.) highlights in particular: from book to bottle.

Whether the documented connection between levels of anxiety and readiness to drink/read operates quite as Wagenbach claims will only be determined when the complications caused by the functionalisation of anxiety have been removed.

Experiments with best-selling novels in America and low-alcohol beer must be considered a failure.

Out of all this follows what we already knew: a culture, which only promotes one aspect – reading or drinking – will sooner or later dry up or drown. Someone who reads too much without wetting his whistle regularly will become stupid; someone who drinks too much without diluting his drink with literature will end up in the gutter. Only the two together preserve culture; only the two together *are* culture.